Waiting for Dolphins

Waiting for Dolphins

Carole Crowe

Boyds Mills Press

I'd like to acknowledge the courage and accomplishment of Tania Aebi, the youngest single-hander to complete a circumnavigation.

And special thanks to my pink-cloud friends in St. Thomas— a writer's group beyond my wildest dreams.

Published by Caroline House
Boyds Mills Press, Inc.
A Highlights Company
815 Church Street
Honesdale, Pennsylvania 18431
Printed in the United States of America

U.S. Cataloging-in-Publication Data
   (Library of Congress Standards)

Crowe, Carole.
    Waiting for Dolphins / by Carole Crowe. 1st ed.
[128]p. :   cm.
Summary: In the aftermath of her father's untimely death,
fifteen-year-old Molly must deal with her grief and the anger toward her
mother.
ISBN 1-56397-847-4
1. Fathers--Death--Fiction--Juvenile literature. 2. Death--
Fiction--Juvenile literature. 3. Mothers and daughters--Fiction--
Juvenile literature. 4. Grief--Fiction--Juvenile literature. [1.
Fathers--Death--Fiction. 2. Death--Fiction. 3. Mothers and
daughters-- Fiction. 4. Grief--Fiction.] I. Title.
813.54 --dc21 [F] 2000   AC   CIP
99-66548

First edition, 2000
The text of this book is set in 12-point Palatino.

10 9 8 7 6 5 4 3 2 1

For my parents, Fran and Charles Horchler

My children, Tara and Darren

*And for always, my husband, Jack,
who sailed me to the dolphins*

One

THE RED SUN HUNG IN THE SKY like a lost carnival balloon, and I wished I could reach up and pull it into my lap. Sitting on the boom, I rested my back against the mast, while the boat drifted at anchor. In spite of the warm trade wind, I shivered and hugged my arms. The horizon was cloudless, the air free of haze. I was sure there would be a green flash, that little bit of color that sometimes appears the moment the sun dips below the earth. I waited—just as Daddy and I had done a million times before.

After storing our luggage below, my mother came up on deck. "Molly," she called. "Molly, where are you?"

Buried low in the folds of the sail, I watched the panic fill her eyes. If I wasn't on the boat, I must be over the side. Always thinking the worst, my mother. Especially now.

"Molly!" she cried as she rushed toward the rail. I gave in before she looked overboard.

"I'm over here," I said in a deliberate, matter-of-fact voice. I kept my eyes on the horizon.

Softly she said, "Molly, do you think it's really a good idea to watch the sunset?"

I closed my eyes, cutting her off.

"Honey, okay. We'll watch it together."

She reached up to rest her hand on my arm, and I pretended to have to scratch my shoulder. She moved her hand away.

The sun was stuck to a cloud and took forever to sink from the sky. I held my breath and waited.

"She's getting close, McGoo," Daddy calls. His laugh is deep and warm, a laugh that always made strangers look over and smile when they heard it.

"A green flash at sunset is God's way of giving the world a touch of the green," he says in his pretend Irish brogue.

"I'm telling you, Jennie," he says to Mom. "God feels sorry for all the poor souls in the world who weren't born Irish. I feel sorry for them! God and I have a lot in common." He laughs and Mom and I lean against his strong shoulders and laugh with him.

"God's Irish, ladies! Here comes the celebration!" And he throws his arms around both of us, as the earth tips to meet the sun, and I pray the sunset will offer up a flash of green for Daddy.

The sun hung motionless until it touched the sea, then began to slide down too quickly. Someone had the end of my red balloon and was dragging it lower and lower. *Here it comes, McGoo,* Daddy whispered in my ear.

Then the sun was gone. And there was nothing. No green flash. No laughter. Just an empty sky.

Everything sounded hollow, like after I'd been swimming under water but hadn't cleared my ears. Like an echo, my mother's voice finally reached me.

". . . don't always get a green flash, Molly. Maybe tomorrow."

"What do you care?" I cried out as I slid off the other side of the boom, away from her. I tripped over the handrail, hitting my head against a stanchion, one of the upright stainless-steel poles that holds our lifelines along the rail.

"Molly, please," she yelled, as I backed away from her. "Let me help you. Your head is bleeding."

I brought my hand down from my forehead and stared at the blood. Tears were pushing up from somewhere deep inside me. *I won't cry*, I thought. *I won't.* I turned and rushed below.

Coming in from the light, the cabin looked dark and dreary, like the funeral parlor near Grandma's house on Long Island. We'd been gone a whole month, and I hardly recognized the boat that had been our home for over six years, since I was eight years old. The rich teak that Mom always lovingly oiled, now looked parched and dead. Peety, the cloth parrot that Daddy insisted he had taught to speak, hung limply from its perch, one wing slightly torn, its colors soiled and washed out. Not even the shelf of our favorite books cheered the cabin.

I took a deep breath, trying to taste my father's special scent, the after-shave that let me find him with my eyes shut once at a party. His scent was gone, along with his laughter.

"Daddy?" I whispered into the empty cabin.

The next morning, I huddled on deck and watched my mother. I tried to stare into her eyes. Read her deepest thoughts.

Startled to see me, as though I were spying, the light left her eyes. "How are you feeling?" she asked.

I shrugged and pulled away the Band-Aid from over my eye. She turned her attention back to the deck, hosing away a month of dirt that had collected in the scuppers.

"I spoke to Roger this morning," Mom said. She coiled the hose around her arm in long loops, her amber eyes pensive, darker than usual. "He made a suggestion."

I was instantly alert.

"He said he wouldn't mind sailing the boat to Florida for us, so we could fly back to New York, instead of—"

"No!"

"He could put his boat in a marina and leave immediately with ours, before any storms—"

"No!"

"Molly, it's too much for us."

"We just got back. And you promised. It's bad enough you want to sell Daddy's boat. The least we can do is sail it back to the States ourselves. In a million years Daddy would never let Roger or anyone else captain it. And *why* do we have to sell it, anyway? Why? You know how much Daddy loved *Emerald Eyes.*"

"We've been all through this." Mom tossed the hose in the locker.

"Fine, we'll sell it!" I said. "But you promised we'd sail the boat back ourselves. And you promised we'd sail to Venezuela first to look for *Magic.* Elizabeth is my best friend." My voice broke.

"I didn't promise. I said 'maybe.' I hadn't thought it through. I never should have agreed to let you come back with me. It's just too upsetting. And we're well into the hurricane season, Molly. It could be dangerous. We shouldn't even be around this part of the Caribbean." She shoved her hands into her hair and squeezed them into fists. It was the same argument she'd had with my father once he'd started drinking again.

"When we get to Venezuela, we'll be safe from hurricanes," I argued. "They never hit at that latitude."

Mom shook her head in annoyance. "It will take *days* to sail there. This boat should be in Venezuela already!"

"Are you going to blame Daddy for dying, too?" I asked softly.

My mother closed her eyes and took a deep breath.

An outboard buzzed and Roger came motoring over in his blue, inflatable dinghy. Unlike our forty-foot fiberglass sloop, he lived aboard a smaller wooden schooner that he had built himself in Maryland at the boatyard his father owned. In all the years we'd known him, he never tired of my father's crazy stories about the police force on Long Island. Like a small boy at a circus, he was mesmerized by Daddy's wild humor.

Roger had been anchored nearby when we got the message about Daddy. He sailed back the next day and walked us to the airport, a small, ragged funeral procession.

He was special, one of our closest cruising friends—at least that's what I'd thought when my father was alive.

I was happy to see him, but I was on guard, too. I couldn't let him take *Emerald Eyes*.

Smiling, he swung alongside our boat and wrapped his hand around my bare foot. The sun lit the hairs on the back of his hand like a golden web.

"Hey, Molly."

"Hey, Roger."

He started to speak, but before he could say something about my father that might make me cry, I pulled my foot away and asked about *Magic*.

Roger shook his head. "Haven't heard a word, Molly. I'm not even sure if they know about—" His eyes met mine, and I looked away quickly. "Nobody knows where they are," he continued.

"It doesn't matter," I said. "We'll find them when we get to Venezuela." I held still, waiting for my mother's reaction.

"Is that what you're doing?" he asked cautiously, looking at my mother. We both waited for her answer.

She exhaled and looked away. "I guess so," she whispered.

"You're sure you don't want me to sail the boat to the States for you?"

"We're *very* sure," I said coldly. "We can sail it ourselves. And we have to see *Magic* anyway."

Roger's face softened. "I understand, Molly. I've been trying to get some information about Elizabeth for you," he said. "Talked to a few cruisers in Venezuela this morning on the ham radio. Nobody has seen *Magic* anywhere. We can't understand it."

Tears welled in my eyes, and I bit down on my bottom lip to stop them. I hadn't let myself cry since Daddy died. I was too afraid that once I started, everything left inside me would spill out like water from a tipped vase.

"Maybe we should take Roger up on his offer," my mother said. "I'm worried about the weather. I'm worried about *you*. What if a hurricane develops before we get to Venezuela? There have already been several in the Gulf."

"But there hasn't been anything in *this* part of the

Caribbean yet," I yelled. "I watched the weather channel at Grandma's. We *have* to see *Magic* before we leave!"

"Stop shouting, Molly. We have to be sensible and do what's safe. We could leave the boat in dry dock here for a few months, take our belongings off the boat, and fly home."

"*Emerald Eyes* is our home," I cried.

"All right, fly to New York," she amended, "and let Roger sail the boat to a broker in Florida when hurricane season is over."

"Mom, you just finished saying we could go to Venezuela. Now two seconds later you're changing your mind?"

My mother closed her eyes, struggling to stay calm. Roger lowered his head and remained silent. Initially my mother had intended to leave me in New York with my grandmother. She wanted to return to the Caribbean alone, sail the boat to Florida immediately, then put it up for sale. But I couldn't give up *Emerald Eyes* without sailing her again. Not so soon after losing Daddy. And I just had to see Elizabeth one more time. After weeks of pleading and arguing, my mother had relented. Now she was going back on her word.

"Mom?"

She sighed heavily. "Okay. We'll get the boat ready. If we get a good weather window, we'll sail to Venezuela. But if a storm develops—"

"Nothing is going to develop." I rushed below, turned on our single-sideband radio, and called into the microphone: "*Magic, Magic, Magic*, this is *Emerald Eyes*." Again, I tried. "*Magic*, come back to *Emerald Eyes*." With the SSB we could talk to someone hundreds, even thousands, of miles away. *Where could they be?* I wondered. *Why hasn't anyone seen them?* Above the static, I heard the low voices of my mother and Roger on deck.

At first I strained to hear, but when she mentioned my father I squeezed my eyes shut and started humming. I could see him standing right in front of me. So real, so close. I reached out to touch him. Then he staggered, and my eyes flew open. Daddy had quit drinking before I was born. Even when I heard him tell funny stories about his drinking days, I knew he took the disease of alcoholism seriously. Wherever we sailed, he attended meetings of Alcoholics Anonymous. Until we got word that Uncle Frank was dead. That's when everything changed.

Uncle Frank wasn't really my uncle, although I loved him like one. He was Daddy's partner, a Nassau County detective, and they'd been best friends since they were boys. The news of his heart attack reached us in St. Thomas. His death was like a hairline crack in our lives. Daddy began hanging out at a dockside bar. For the first time ever, my parents fought. And then my family shattered like a fragile Christmas ball.

Scanning radio frequencies, I tried *Magic* again. If only I could talk to Elizabeth. I missed her parents, too, even her little brother, Jason, the most annoying human being in the universe. But where were they?

We rolled in the wake of a passing boat, and Peety's perch swung toward me. With the tip of my finger, I tapped the bird's beak and he flipped upside down. I righted him, flapped his wings with my fingers, then kissed the top of his head.

On deck, I heard my mother laugh at something Roger said. How could she laugh so soon after my father's death? Her voice sounded gentle, the way she used to speak to my father. My fingernails dug half-moons in the palms of my hands.

Maybe if she had talked to my father that way—

But no, after Daddy started drinking, all she did was worry and complain. Wanted us to leave St. Thomas, get far away from the bars. Wanted me to go to those stupid Al-Anon meetings with her, for the relatives of alcoholics. I tore up the pamphlets she gave me and tossed them to the wind. Daddy needed to know somebody was on his side. She wouldn't even let us sail to Trinidad again to meet *Magic* for Carnival. Too much drinking there, too. Nervous Nelly— that's what my father called her.

Well, we left St. Thomas, and what did all her worrying get us? A memory of the last days flashed in my mind. Trembling, I shook it away.

My mother murmured something to Roger, and I leaned closer to watch her through the port. She was lifting her head from his shoulder. My mouth went dry. Tenderly, he pressed a folded white handkerchief under her eyes. She'd been crying, not laughing. Crying on Roger's shoulder.

Gazing into his eyes, my mother said, "I know you had to change your sailing plans for us, Roger. You should be safely in Venezuela. I'm sorry, but I thank you for everything."

"Don't be sorry, Jennie," he whispered. "I'm right where I'm supposed to be—with you. I'm still willing to sail the boat to the States right now if you change your mind."

"Thanks, Roger." She lowered her voice even more. "I'd love the help. I want to sell it as soon as possible. But Molly—" I couldn't see her face, just the shrug of her shoulders.

"Yes, I know," he said. "There's another possibility, Jennie. If you do go to Venezuela, I could sail *with* you to Florida when you leave. The three of us. Would that make things easier? "

The three of us? Roger instead of my father? I dragged my fingernails down my cheeks. My face felt like it was filled with Novocain.

"Oh, Roger, that's so sweet of you. I might take you up on it."

My hands closed into fists.

"You could come back to the Caribbean afterwards, Jennie. Stay on *Golden Slippers*, relax in the sun. You and Molly."

My chest was aching. I could barely swallow.

"Oh God, that sounds heavenly. I wish the boat were sold already. I just want to be done with it." Sighing, she lowered her head to his shoulder and closed her eyes.

I stumbled backwards, dizzy and sick to my stomach. *"I just want to be done with it,"* I repeated. Be done with *Emerald Eyes*. Be done with my father.

At that moment I hated her so much—hated her and loved my father—I wanted to rush on deck, beat her with my fists, and kill Roger the way my father had died. I wanted to make her pay for everything that happened.

When Roger finally left, she came below.

"Molly, we need to talk."

I glared, but said nothing.

"Why are you so mad at me? Why?"

I could taste the anger in my throat. "I wish *you* had died," I said.

She shook me roughly, then let go quickly as though she'd burned her hands.

"You listen to me—"

"No, I *won't* listen. Not again. I listened once and now Daddy's dead. It's all your fault. You killed him!" There, I'd said it.

Her head flew back like she'd been struck. Unable to look at the pain on her face, I closed my eyes. *You killed him! You!* The words screamed in my head just like they had since we learned of my father's death.

Her voice was a mere whisper. "What are you talking about?"

"You know exactly what I'm talking about! Nagging him constantly about AA meetings. Fighting with him. He told you he didn't need AA, that he'd just lost his best friend. If you'd left him alone, stopped picking on him for two seconds—"

"He was going to bars—"

"So what! He wasn't drinking, was he? You and that stupid Al-Anon meditation book. Reading it in his face. Going to those meetings and making him feel bad. *You* made him drink. *You* made him go away."

She didn't say a word. She didn't have to. I thought guilt was written all over her face. But even then, even when my anger toward her was so deep it hurt to breathe, I knew it wasn't completely her fault. My terrible secret burned like a hot stone in my heart: My mother had driven him away—but it was *my* fault Daddy was dead.

THE NEXT MORNING I AWOKE to the pale sky
above me. A heron winged across my vision. I thought I
had turned to cloud and floated up from my bunk.
Floated through the open hatch, right into the sky. I
closed my eyes and drifted.

*Daddy stands alone at the bow. His dark hair is shaggy,
needing one of Mom's haircuts, and his white cotton shirt bil-
lows in back like a sail as the wind catches underneath. He's
leaning against the bow rail with one leg resting on a stainless
bar, and I can see the jagged scar across his knee, the injury that
made him leave the police force. He doesn't hear us creep up
behind him. Mom hooks her arm around my neck and buries
kisses in my hair. Surprised by my giggles, Daddy turns. His
smile is white against his bronze skin. His blues eyes sparkle
with laughter.*

When I opened my eyes I was smiling, too. Then a
small cry caught in my throat. I squeezed my eyes shut
to recapture the memory, to make it real so I could see the

love in his eyes. But it was gone. And there was no way I could ever bring it back.

The first sound I heard was my mother's whisper, "Molly, you awake?"

I almost answered, but remembered my anger in time. When I heard our outboard, I quickly poked my head from the hatch. There she was, motoring over to Roger's boat for coffee. Just like she and my father used to do. Just like nothing had changed.

The wind came up later that afternoon and small whitecaps peaked across the harbor. A colony of jellyfish drifted by like purple parachutes. I unclipped my auburn hair, letting the curls fall around my face and bounce below my shoulders. Mom stepped to the edge of the deck just above the swim ladder and dived, the turquoise water so clear I watched her all the way to the bottom. I glanced toward *Golden Slippers* to see if Roger was watching her, too. He was. A sketch pad in his lap, he was drawing intently, and every now and then he'd look over, then go back to his pad. My mother broke the surface, her hair plastered over her face like a child's ready for a haircut.

She pushed her hair back with both hands. "You better come in and bathe before it gets cool," she called to me.

I didn't answer. She began her slow crawl around the boat. Never losing rhythm, she snapped her hair to the side each time she turned her face for air. In spite of my anger, I couldn't help but notice how beautiful she was, as graceful as a dolphin.

"Mommy, how come I have to swing my arms so many times to swim? How come I keep sinking?"

"Try it again, Molly. I'll keep my hand on your stomach. Go ahead, I've got you."

The memory left a cold spot on my stomach, as though a warm hand had been taken away.

I saw Roger look up. I lowered myself into the water and used the ladder to hold myself below the surface. *How can I stop her from selling* Emerald Eyes? I wondered. I stayed underwater to make the lonely feeling go away, to make Roger go away. I surfaced, gasping for air, and climbed back on deck. I liked the strange feel of my wet hair down my back, long and straight instead of curly. It made me feel like I was someone else. Anyone else but Molly.

I washed my body and hair with Joy. When we first left New York, my old friends felt sorry for me because I had to bathe with a dish detergent that lathered in salt water, but I loved the clean, lemony smell. I held my nose and jumped in the water, my soapy hair drifting on the surface like the laundry some island women wash at the river. I pulled myself up and down, churning like a washer on rinse. *What'ya think, McGoo? The Caribbean Sea is your own private bubble bath. Nothing's too good for my little* Emerald Eyes. Bubbles, frothy and white, drifted around my face, and I blew them away from my stinging eyes and climbed back on deck.

I let the sun-warmed fresh water run from the red nozzle on the black shower bag into my mouth and eyes and rinsed the salt from my body and hair. Moments later I heard my mother climb on deck. I kept the towel draped over my face, breathing slowly in and out, smelling the darkness.

"I can't stand the way Roger is gawking," I said.

"How could you possibly know what Roger is doing

with a towel over your face? And he's drawing, for heaven's sake, like he always does."

A sail flapped nearby, and I dragged the towel from my head. A windsurfer swung his sail around to pull away from our boat. His hair, dark like Daddy's, was a little too long, and it fell across one of his eyes. His skin was golden from the sun. I couldn't tell his age for sure, but he looked older than me, eighteen or maybe more. His body was lanky, but his shoulders looked strong, like he was a boy on the cusp of becoming a man. He didn't look directly at us, but I could tell he knew we were watching. He tried to swing the sail around, but the wind shifted suddenly, and he lost his balance and fell into the water. Quickly he looked back, checking to see if I'd seen him fall.

Mom saw me watching him and walked closer, rubbing her arm with a thick white towel. "He must be off that black catboat that just sailed in," she said. "Wonder what happened to it?" The boat was beamy, much wider than ours. A long gouge marred the whole length of one side.

The windsurfer finally managed to stand. He slipped his feet into the straps on the white board, slowly pulled the heavy sail out of the water by the long uphaul cord, and shook it until it caught the wind. He turned back once to see if I was still watching.

A stiff gust of wind filled his rainbow-colored sail, and he leaned back, away from the board and sail, to build up speed. He headed outside the reef that protected the anchorage and tacked into open water, sailing back and forth off the wind. Then he swung the sail around the front of the board.

"Oh my gosh!" I cried, as he headed directly toward

the exposed reef. Brown, jagged coral cut through the surface of the water like broken teeth. The coral, always exposed in that section of the reef, was almost impossible to pass over. But every now and then, because the wind was up, a gust would blow a small, foamy wave over the top.

Mom turned when she heard me cry out. "What is he doing?" she yelled. "He'll be ripped to pieces if he falls. Hey! Hey!" She jumped up onto the cabin top, waving her arms to warn him off. "Doesn't he see the reef? What's wrong with him?"

There was no way to know when a gust of wind might push enough water over the reef to make it possible for the sailboard to surf over it. But he didn't seem to care. He leaned his whole body out from the board, pulled on the wishbone boom around the sail to increase his speed. A double row of ragged teeth lined his path like the open mouth of a shark. I covered my face and peeked through my fingers as he surfed dead into the coral. As if his life were charmed, a small wave formed and carried him inches over the top. Then he raced by *Emerald Eyes*, gave me a big smile, and winked. Winked, just like Daddy used to do.

"Yeah," I whispered. My heart was pounding like crazy, and my legs felt like rubber.

My mother went nuts.

"That kid is absolutely insane." She grabbed her towel and charged back to the cockpit. "He could have been killed! It's a miracle he wasn't, coming over an exposed reef like that."

"But he wasn't killed," I said breathlessly. "Was he? He wasn't even hurt. So what's the big deal?"

"What's the big deal?" Mom stared at me like I had lost

my mind. "What's the big deal? Someone deliberately does something that almost kills him and you ask 'What's the big deal?' Are you serious?" She edged toward me, her lips as tight as two wires.

"Yes, I'm serious," I said. "I don't understand why you're getting so crazy over it." But, of course, I did understand. I understood perfectly. To be honest, I thought the surfer's stunt was foolish, too, but my mother's reaction made me defend him, like I'd tried to defend my father. And once I started, I didn't know how to stop.

White blotches appeared on her cheeks. "I'm getting *crazy*, as you call it, because that boy almost got killed. But I'm even more upset by *your* attitude. You really think it's okay to do something so stupid? It's *not* okay, Molly. It's not okay to put yourself in danger. Or anyone else, for that matter."

"I think it's great that he wasn't afraid, okay!" My lip was quivering. "And I don't think it's fair to criticize someone just because they aren't a . . . a *Nervous Nelly* over every minor thing."

"Minor?" she whispered. Her eyes filled with tears. And I guess we both knew our fight wasn't about the windsurfer.

I spun around, raced below, and changed quickly. I slathered sunblock all over my face so I wouldn't turn into a freckled rust bucket. I stuffed the shopping list and money in my pocket and pulled my father's canvas hat from a locker. I pressed the hat to my face and drew in a deep breath. The smell of mildew tickled my nose. My eyes teared. I jammed the hat on, stuffed my wet hair up and tightened the slipknot under my chin.

When I climbed on deck, Mom was at the bow repairing the green starboard running light. We needed the green and red lights to sail at night so other boats could see us and tell which way we were heading. Mom refused to sail at night unless every single light was okay. Nervous Nelly.

"I'm going ashore," I said, climbing into the dinghy.

She turned and a little sound escaped her lips. The color drained from her face. She walked toward me until her feet were eye-level with my face. "For a minute you looked just like—" She didn't finish. Crouching on the deck, she sat back on her heels, her bent knees white against her tanned skin. Gently, she straightened the brim of the hat and brushed her thumb along the stiff outer edge.

She was so close I could smell her minty breath, see the beads of sweat across her upper lip. Our eyes locked. We didn't hear Roger's engine until he was alongside *Emerald Eyes*.

My mother smiled at him. "Come on up," she said, standing.

I doubt he even noticed that I didn't say hello.

"Did you take the money?" my mother asked me.

I nodded.

She took Roger's line. "Let's hope it's enough. I can't believe the prices around here. Worse than Long Island." She shook her head suddenly. "Oh what *difference* does it make?" Daddy used to tease her all the time for worrying about money. He said we had more than enough with the savings from the sale of the house and his pension. Yet she always insisted we give an accounting of every cent we'd spent so she could mark it in our finance log. There was even a special column for ice cream, because Daddy enjoyed it so. "It's cheaper than booze, Jennie," he'd say, laughing. And he was right. Nothing ever cost us more.

Roger climbed into the cockpit and sat at the helm. He

propped his bare foot against the wooden ship's wheel that Daddy loved—the wheel I'd once sanded for him when I still thought I could make things right. Watching Roger, remembering my father, tears of rage filled my eyes.

It had been early one morning, before daylight. With all its curves and ridges and spokes, sanding the wheel was difficult, but it needed a new coat of varnish. Determined to fix our lives, I sanded and sanded until my father woke up.

"Look!" I cried. "It's all done, Daddy. All ready to varnish. And I even used two different grits like you taught me." But he didn't smile or say, "Nice job, McGoo." He didn't say a word. Just stared at my face, dusty and streaked with tears. Then he drew me tightly to his chest and kissed the top of my head. He left the boat and didn't return for two days. When he came back, he'd been drinking for the first time. And that was the beginning of the end.

Now Roger was at the helm. Trying to replace my father. Trying to steal his life. Roger and my mother, conspiring to be done with him. I gunned the outboard engine and left a rooster tail of water behind the dinghy. The wind bit into my face. Speeding away from them, I made a vow—a vow that I would keep even if it killed me. "Don't worry, Daddy," I whispered. "I'll never let her sell *Emerald Eyes*."

Three

On THE WAY BACK FROM SHOPPING, the heavy canvas bag dug into my shoulder. Earlier I'd walked the long way around to avoid a shark pool, the hotel's tourist attraction. The sharks had never frightened me, but that's where I'd had my last conversation with Daddy, and still I couldn't bear to think of the terrible thing I'd done the next day.

Now the sharks seemed to beckon me.

One side of the walk bordered the shark pool, and on the other was a steep drop onto rocks. My mouth was dry as I stepped on the narrow walkway. *Daddy is drunk. He staggers. Gray nurse sharks pressed their heads against the side of the cement pool that kept them captive. Their long tails were fanned out like a deck of Tarot cards predicting a dark future. Again Daddy teeters and one foot slips into the shark pool. I'm not afraid, and I rush to help him. He says there's something important he wants to tell me.*

Remembering that night, the ice bag fell into the crook of my arm and pulled me off balance. I let it drop to the walk and put my arms out to regain my balance.

That's when I saw someone coming toward me from the other end of the walk, someone who looked like my father. His head was framed in the center of the dying sun. The glare hid his face. His white shirt sleeves were rolled to his elbows. My scalp prickled and my knees weakened. I strained to see better. I knew it couldn't be my father. And yet—

"*Daddy?*" I whispered. Suddenly, he laughed, then teetered wildly like he was drunk. Dark spots appeared before my eyes. I felt myself falling. I slipped into the memory of my last talk with Daddy by the shark pool.

"Hey, McGoo, I want you to come with me when I help that guy deliver the boat. It'll be good blue-water experience for you." My father's voice is thick with drink. "We'll leave your mother here. Be back in a couple of weeks. Give her a short vacation from us." He grins and his blue eyes crease at the sides like soft leather.

"I'll watch over my little girl. And you can take care of your old dad. What do you say?"

My hands feel damp and I rub them on my shorts. What if he gets drunk when we're in the middle of the ocean? How will he watch over me then? "Sure, Daddy," I answer weakly. "Just you and me."

"Are you okay? You look like you've seen a ghost."

I felt the blush burn my cheeks as I found myself sitting on the walk, the windsurfer leaning over me. "Hey, I know you," he said, smiling. "You're the girl from that boat, *Emerald Eyes.*" He tried to help me stand, but I wouldn't get up. "What's wrong? Did you have a dizzy spell?"

I shook his arms away and took a deep breath. "No, I did *not* have a dizzy spell. You . . . you looked like my . . . Oh, forget it. I thought you were falling in with the sharks. It made me lose my balance, that's all."

"I was just fooling around. Didn't mean to scare you." When he plopped down in front of me, I felt even dumber.

"Well, you *did* scare me," I snapped.

Grinning, he said, "Wow! I see where your boat got its name. Your eyes really get green when you're mad." He straightened my hat and tugged on a loose tendril.

"You *also* scared me when you were windsurfing!" I could hear my mother's voice coming out of my mouth and felt the heat rise in my face again. Softening my tone, I said, "Didn't you see us trying to warn you off the reef?"

He paused, then slapped his forehead dramatically. "Warn me *off*? I thought you were cheering me *on*!" When he grinned, his blue eyes sparkled, and I almost smiled. The chip in his front tooth made him look more like a little boy than someone older than me. Gingerly, I stood up on the walk and hitched the bag on my shoulder. One of the sharks was swimming back and forth.

Still shaky from the memory of the last night with my father, I let the windsurfer walk backwards in front of me, holding my outstretched hands, until he led me off the walkway. "You're not still mad are you?" he asked. "I'm sorry I scared you." This time his face was so sincere, I couldn't stay mad.

"Molly! Molly!" My mother came running up the dock.

"Molly," he whispered. "Nice name." His back was to my mother, and he leaned close and kissed me quickly on the nose.

My mother almost knocked him over when she pushed between us. "Are you all right? What happened? Why are you holding your nose?"

"Mom, you're embarrassing me."

"One of the sharks scared her," the windsurfer lied. "I caught her just before she fell in."

She glared at the front of the bright, pink hotel. "Sharks, of all things. I have never heard of such a ridiculous idea."

"Hey, it's cool," he said. "They're just nurse sharks. It's a great tourist attraction."

Mom spun around and glared at him. My father used to say the same thing. "You!" she said in a tight voice, finally recognizing him. "You're the one who sailed over that reef today!"

"Mom," I pleaded. "Please."

"Ma'am, I never even saw that reef until it was too late." He was such a good liar his eyes didn't even flicker.

"You didn't see us trying to warn you?"

"No, ma'am, I surely didn't. But thank you kindly. I'll know better next time." He put his hand out and introduced himself, trying to win my mother over with good manners. "Christopher Barrett, ma'am. Sorry if I frightened you."

My mother hesitated, then shook his hand. "Jennie McGuire," she said without enthusiasm.

"Chris! Shake a leg," a voice called. A creepy-looking sailor, much older than Christopher, was waiting at the end of the dock. A beer belly pulled his T-shirt up short, revealing a fold of flabby skin. His hair was black with streaks of gray, and he wore it tied at the back of his neck in a ponytail.

"Gotta go," Christopher said. "Nice meeting you, Ms. McGuire. You too, Molly." He backed away, his blue eyes sparkling with laughter. When my mother turned from him, he winked at me, then jogged toward his friend.

"Mom, did you have to be so rude?" I asked her.

She ignored the question. "Are you sure you're all right? Why were you sitting on the walk?"

"Why did you come ashore?"

"I thought you might need help with the groceries. Roger brought me in."

My back stiffened.

"There's something else, Molly. We may have a problem. A storm system has formed off the coast of Africa, a strong tropical wave that might strengthen."

I huffed. "So what?" I said. "It's only a *wave*; it's not even a depression yet. It still has to turn into a tropical storm before it ever gets as bad as a hurricane. And it's still off *Africa*, nowhere near us. It won't become a hurricane, anyway. They never do."

"They most *certainly* do," she said. "I don't want to take any chances, Molly."

"Mom, it's only a tropical wave. Don't get so uptight. It'll peter out, and if it doesn't, it'll blow out to sea like most others. Stop worrying."

"Roger suggested—"

"Roger, Roger, Roger! I don't care what he suggested. What is he all of a sudden, Mr. High Seas? Daddy was a better sailor than him a million times over!"

"Well, your father's dead and Roger isn't!"

Fruit and vegetables rolled from the canvas bag when it dropped from my shoulder. My mother's hand flew to her mouth, as if she couldn't believe she'd spoken the words.

"I hate you," I said.

"I'm sorry, Molly . . . I didn't mean it the way it sounded."

"You meant it exactly the way it sounded."

"I am *not* the enemy here, Molly. Will you please stop fighting me?"

"Why? So you and Roger can—"

"Hey, Moll, need some help?" We both turned at the sound of his voice. Approaching with a smile, he scooped up a papaya and two yams.

I ran past him, jumped into the dinghy, and roared away, leaving them side by side.

Later when Mom called through the door about dinner, I pretended to be asleep. Finally, she gave up. *I have to stop fighting with her*, I thought, *or I'll never talk her into keeping* Emerald Eyes. But what if she won't listen to me? What if nothing I say makes her change her mind?

I turned on the light and rifled through my locker for something to read. I took out a book, *Maiden Voyage*, by Tania Aebi. It was my father's last gift to me, and I hadn't even read it. Seeing his handwriting brought tears to my eyes. "For Molly on her 14th birthday. To the bravest sailor in the world." The words filled me with shame. I hadn't been brave. The one time my father needed me, I'd been a coward. And he was dead because of it.

Far into the night, I read about Tania Aebi's adventure as the youngest person to sail around the world alone. An idea began to grow, slowly at first, like a sprout unfolding from a bean, then as wild as a weed.

I felt a rush of fear and a tingle of excitement. If Tania Aebi could sail around the world by herself, why couldn't I sail away on *Emerald Eyes*?

The thought took my breath away. I hugged the book to my chest. How strange that my father had given me this particular book for my birthday. Had he sensed, in some mystical way, that he'd be leaving me? I thought of his last words to me: "Take care of *Emerald Eyes*." I almost cried, then began to laugh. For the first time since his death, I felt my father's presence, felt him showing me how to save *Emerald Eyes*. And how to save myself.

Four

EARLY THE NEXT MORNING, I awoke to the sound of pelicans dive-bombing head-first around our boat. Mom was still in her cabin. I crept up the stairs. The varnished hatch was closed against night showers, and I opened it to let the air cool the cabin. I drummed a pencil against a notebook. What would I have to do to sail away by myself?

I gazed at *Emerald Eyes* and tried to picture myself alone on the ocean. Nervously, I tapped my bare feet on the teak deck. The white cabin top glistened with morning dew, and I printed my name in it: *Captain Molly*. Quickly I wiped the wet letters away. Shielding my eyes, I looked to the top of the mast, over fifty feet high. My stomach fell. Once while we were at sea, my mother and I had hauled my father up in a bosun's chair to retrieve a lost halyard. A chill went through me, and my fingertips tingled. Heights had never bothered me, until after my father's funeral. If it hadn't been for my panic-attack while crossing a bridge with my grandmother, I wouldn't have known about my new fear. Would I ever have to go up the mast?

One other fear made my knees weak. Would I run into horrible storms like Tania did? I shook myself. I was getting like my mother, worrying about things that might never happen. My fear of heights was probably just a reaction to the funeral. I bet I was already over it. Still, I'd better find out in a safe harbor instead of in the middle of the ocean. Although we'd never used them, somewhere on the boat we had canvas mast steps that slid up the mast in the mainsail track.

I made the first entry in my notebook: "Find the mast steps."

I heard my mother at the stove below and smelled the coffee brewing. A few minutes later, she climbed into the cockpit with a steaming mug. Not seeing me on deck, she sighed and closed her eyes, ringed with deep circles, then pressed the warm cup against her cheek. When her eyes slowly opened, they glistened with tears. *Was she remembering my father? Or thinking of Roger?*

Seeing me startled her, and she quickly brushed a tear away. I thought she looked guilty. "Molly, I didn't know you were up. I overslept and didn't get weather. Did you listen?"

I gave my head a slight shake.

"Maybe Roger got it. Have you seen him on deck yet?"

Turning away, I didn't answer.

She sat down next to me. "Molly, look at me." She took my chin and I tried to resist. "We have to stop tearing into each other like we did yesterday. It only makes everything so much worse. For both of us. I think we should talk about your feelings, about what's going on between us." She brushed a wisp of hair from my face.

I swallowed the lump forming in my throat. I didn't want to talk about my feelings. How could I talk about them when I didn't even know what they were?

"What's to talk about?" I said. "You and Roger want to sell my father's boat as fast as you can." I shrugged. "No problem. I don't care anymore. Whatever you want to do is fine with me."

"I know you're upset."

"I'm not upset." *Not anymore,* I thought. "Why don't you go visit *Roger* and check on the weather. I'm sure he knows everything, right down to the last gust of wind."

"Look." Her tone was sharp. "I know how hard this is for you, Molly, but I'm not going to let you go on like this. Abusing me, hurting yourself. You're not the only one in pain . . ." Unable to go on, she pushed her hand through her hair. A drop of coffee splashed on my knee. I flicked it away.

"Jennie! Did you get weather?" Roger called from his boat.

Mom called back, "No, did you?"

"Yes, want me to come over?"

"I'll come to you," she answered. Standing, she touched my shoulder. "You want to come with me?" I shrugged her hand away.

Before she left, she hesitated, then said, "About your school work, Molly—"

"No problem." I reached for the notebook. "I've already started a project." I studied through a correspondence school, and because my schooling had to fit in with cruising, I usually continued through the summer. But I hadn't opened a book in over a month.

"Good. I'm glad you're feeling up to it. If you need help—"

"I've got everything under control," I said.

My mother climbed into the dinghy and motored over to Roger.

Once I had loved her and Daddy more than anything in the whole world. Loved them so much, I had promised never to leave them. "I want that in writing," Daddy had said. "Get the paper, Jen, hurry. If she tries to leave us, we'll take her to court." My mother had pulled me into her lap, laughing.

I didn't realize my eyes were closed, my fingers touching the cheek she'd kissed, until Christopher yelled, "Hey, Molly, got a toothache?"

He was windsurfing toward the reef again, and I leaped to my feet. At the last moment, he jibed the sail around instead. Grinning, he called out, "You have to learn to trust me!"

My mother was watching from Roger's boat. I smiled at Christopher and waved hard until she turned away. Christopher whizzed past without stopping.

I worked quickly and emptied the cockpit locker of coiled lines, the hose, cans of paint and varnish, but I didn't find the mast steps. Where had my parents stored that bag? Next I searched the lockers in the cabin. No luck. I pulled up floorboards and searched the bilge. Sweat dripped from my nose. Twice I stopped searching when I heard an outboard coming near. But I should have known my mother wouldn't be hurrying back. At last I found them. Great. But would I have the courage to climb fifty feet? There was only one way to find out. Before I took the boat, I'd have to go up the mast.

"*Magic, Magic, Magic,* this is *Emerald Eyes.*" *Where could they be?* I wondered. Making friends was the hardest thing about living on a boat. When my father had been shot on duty, my parents decided to leave Long Island to sail away and show me the world so I might grow up in a safer environment, away from violence and drugs. I loved living on a sailboat, studying through a correspondence school. Keeping friends was the only hard part. Trying to rendezvous every few months, never seeing some friends again who sailed to Europe or the South Pacific.

Elizabeth and her family were from Canada and had planned on sailing around the world when we met them three years earlier. They put their plans on hold because Elizabeth and I became friends. But where was she now? What if her family heard about my father and figured we weren't coming back to the Caribbean? Had they continued their circumnavigation? Would I ever see Elizabeth again?

I grabbed the mike. "*Magic, Magic,* this is *Emerald Eyes*. Do you copy?" The static was steady. I thought about the first time we'd met in Bonaire, one of the Dutch Caribbean Islands. Anchored across the harbor from us, the four of them were lined up along the deck of their boat, facing the water like a ship's honor guard, except they were all wearing bathing suits. Even with binoculars, we couldn't figure out what they were doing. Every few seconds one of them would lean over the side, then stand straight, then another would bend and straighten, sometimes the same person twice—as if a puppeteer was releasing the lines, then yanking them up tight.

Up . . . down . . . up . . . down.

Dad let out a whoop when we neared their boat in our

dinghy. Mom and I cracked up, too. They were eating slices of watermelon, bending at the waist to spit the seeds over the side.

The memory made me grin.

A voice broke through the static and my heart flipped, but it wasn't *Magic*.

A gust of wind blew across the boat and rocked it gently. I smiled again, picturing the whole family lined up, spitting seeds. Elizabeth was my age, but she was taller than me, the only one in her family with dark hair. Three years ago when we met, her body was already getting curvy. It took me a while to catch up. Like her father, she had jokey-looking brown eyes. I got the distinct impression she was sizing me up.

And then there was Jason, five years younger than us. The sun lit his blond, wispy hair from behind, and he had the most angelic face I'd ever seen—until he shot a watermelon seed through the space where he'd lost a front tooth. It smacked against my white T-shirt and sat there like a shiny, black bug.

From two people down, Karl leaned over and stared at him.

"It shot out accidentally, Dad," Jason said. "Honest."

I plucked the seed from my shirt and held it against my middle finger with my thumb, planning to hit him right between the eyes. Dad said, "Molly" in his I'm-not-kidding voice.

Elizabeth narrowed her eyes at me. "I hope you weren't about to pick on my little brother." She smiled at him sweetly—and shot him with a seed.

Elizabeth and I were instant friends.

I tried *Magic* on our VHF radio, which had a much shorter range than the single sideband. They'd never hear it as far away as Venezuela, but I needed to try something. Of course, they didn't answer.

Leaving both radios on, I flipped through cruising guides from the many islands we'd visited in the Caribbean. I didn't intend to sail around the world like Tania Aebi, but I still had to sail far enough away so my mother couldn't find me.

If I stayed in the Caribbean, someone might recognize the boat. I tossed the cruising guide aside and picked up another. Where else could I go? Europe? I wiggled my nose against Peety's beak. "What do you think, buddy? Any ideas?" He didn't talk to me like he did my father.

I closed my eyes and thought about the places Tania had gone. *Where do you want me to go, Daddy?* The answer was so clear he might have whispered in my ear. Of course—Tahiti! Tania loved the islands in the Pacific. And didn't Daddy always say he wanted to go to Tahiti? It was Mom who didn't want us to sail across the Pacific Ocean. It's too far, she said. What if Molly needs a doctor? Nervous Nelly. The South Pacific was a perfect destination. Like Mom, even Roger didn't want to go there, so I wouldn't have to worry about running into them. *Them.* Already I was thinking of Roger and my mother as a couple.

I pulled several charts from the locker and unfurled one. I would have to go through the Panama Canal. Maybe I could stop at the Galapagos! See the boobies with blue feet and swim with turtles and dolphins. I scribbled a reminder in my notebook to buy more charts and guidebooks. I slid a band from another chart and flattened it on the navigation table. The Pacific Ocean. My heart thumped as I stared at all the white space between specks of land. White space that represented open water. My fingers left damp snakes on the paper.

I could do it, couldn't I? I'd never sailed alone, but neither had Tania when she sailed out of New York Harbor. And my father wouldn't have given me the book if he didn't think I could do it. Hadn't he always said I was the best sailor he knew? I let go of the chart, and it snapped shut like a window shade. But sailing alone was the least of my problems. How could I take *Emerald Eyes* without getting caught by my mother? Suppose I never got the chance to sail away before we left Venezuela for Florida? I needed an alternate plan. If we sailed to Florida to sell the boat, my mother would have to leave it with a broker. That's when I could take it. I could even empty my savings account there. It would be easier to leave from the Caribbean, so much closer to the Panama Canal, but if I had to sail from Florida, I'd do it. Whatever it took, I'd do it.

Hearing my mother pull up, I shoved the charts away and hid the mast steps in the locker under my bunk.

She was already talking as she climbed into the cabin. "They've upgraded that system to a depression, Molly. The weather service is sending a plane up later today." For a moment she avoided my eyes, then faced me. "We can't go to Venezuela with this depression. I'm sorry."

I watched her in silence.

"Roger's calling a yacht broker he knows in the Virgin Islands. We'll sail back to St. Thomas and leave the boat there."

"St. Thomas!" My face was burning. St. Thomas was too close. I needed more time. "That's not fair! What about *Magic*?"

"I said we'd go to Venezuela if a storm didn't develop. Everything's changed now. Roger offered to sail with us to St. Thomas, but I can't let him do that. We have his boat to worry about, too."

My anger grew like a bubble of hot liquid glass. "How much time do I . . . do we have?"

"We'll leave at first light for St. Thomas. With these winds we can be there in a few days, give the boat to a broker, and fly right to the States."

"It's only a tropical depression, not a hurricane! It will probably break up or blow out to sea. Why do we have to leave in the morning? Why can't we wait and see? You promised we could sail to Venezuela and look for *Magic*!"

"If the depression strengthens, we may not be able to go to Venezuela *or* the Virgin Islands. I want to leave while we still have a chance."

"Let's just wait and see what happens. *Please.*"

She blinked slowly. "No, Molly. I know how you feel, but this whole thing is too much for us."

The hot bubble in my chest exploded. "Too much for *you!*"

"Yes, all right, too much for me! I thought maybe, coming back, it might be healing . . . but—"

"Fine," I said. "Suit yourself. No problem." I'd been gripping Peety's perch and accidentally ripped it down. I scooped him up and raced to my cabin. When my mother tapped on the door, I scrambled on deck through my hatch.

Alone at the bow, I fought back tears. *I can't give up* Emerald Eyes, I thought. *Not in a few days. Not in a million years.* Staring into space, it was a long time before the snap of color caught my eye. A giant red and white flag, a maple leaf in the center, fluttered from a boat's backstay. A Canadian flag. I stared at the boat in disbelief—a smile stretching across my face. *Magic* was sailing through the harbor.

Five

"Mom!" I SHOUTED, forgetting myself in the excitement.

She rushed on deck. Awkwardly I pointed.

Jason spotted us first. For the longest time he just stared at *Emerald Eyes*, like he couldn't believe it either. Then he sprinted toward his father at the helm. Instantly, the boat altered course, and Elizabeth appeared on deck with her mother. They circled us twice, everyone waving, at first frantically, then self-consciously because I wasn't waving back. I was trying too hard not to cry.

Karl called out, "How's the holding ground here?"

"There are some rocky spots over there. Anchor right next to us," Mom shouted.

I was filled with excitement when we eventually motored over, seeing Elizabeth, seeing all of them, even Jason, but as soon as we boarded and I looked into their troubled faces, I didn't know how to act.

Gina wrapped her arms around Mom, and Karl started toward me. I must have turned to stone right before his eyes because he stopped suddenly. "Oh, Molly, Molly, what do I say to you?" I'd never seen him so upset. Jason was staring at me, about to cry. He ran toward my mother, hugged her tightly, and buried his head against her waist.

Elizabeth watched me from the companionway. I held my breath knowing I'd die if even she tried to hug me.

"I'll get the tea ready," Karl murmured. In the cabin below, I heard him blowing his nose loudly.

"Jennie, we just found out about Danny," Gina said. "We had engine trouble and had to haul the boat. Then we took a trip instead of staying on board while it was being repaired. The radio isn't hooked up. Oh, listen to me babble."

Jason wiggled out of my mother's embrace, his eyes still wet.

"I just finished a letter to you and Molly. I was going to send it to your mailing service. I didn't know where you were. We couldn't believe it when Jason saw your boat."

Jason picked at the hem of his bathing trunks, his blond hair spilling around his ears. He shifted his eyes toward me, then away.

"I thought you were in Venezuela by now," my mother said.

"We would have been, but for the engine trouble," Karl answered, climbing up with a plate of cookies. "We just talked to someone who knows Roger and found out he was here. Have you heard about this depression?"

Elizabeth and I still hadn't said a word. In the past, we would be hugging, talking at the same time. Slowly she moved toward me. Her hair was different, short and spiky. Beaded braids hung from her bangs.

I heard Gina's voice. "Oh Jennie, I'm so sorry. We're all so sorry." She wrapped her arms around my mother again. "We loved Danny so much." And she began to cry. Then Mom began to cry, too.

Elizabeth took my wrist and I followed her below, Jason scrambling after us. In the cabin, I stopped short by the framed photograph he'd taken of my father, holding up an egg and grinning at the camera. Behind the frame, Jason had stuck a long scarlet feather with a velvet-black tip. Anchored together near a scarlet ibis rookery, we'd all collected feathers every morning after the birds flew off for the day. As hard as I'd tried, I never found one with a black tip like Jason's. The day *Magic* left us, Daddy yelled over, "This is an ibis egg, Jase. We're raising our own feathers!" My eyes filled with tears, remembering his laughter.

Jason snatched the feather from the frame and hid it behind his back.

Gina must have seen the three of us staring at the photograph. She bustled down the stairs. "Come, children," she said. "Come up and have some cookies with us. Everything will be all right." Behind us the kettle whistled loudly.

Once we were in the cockpit, no one seemed to know what to say. Finally Jason broke the ice. "Look what I bought, Molly." He was holding something that hung from a leather cord around his neck. A tiny dead shark floated in a tube of liquid, its skin, white and wrinkled, something only Jason would want.

Elizabeth poked me in the arm. "Notice the incredible likeness between the *boy* and the *thing*?"

Looking at the shark, then at Jason, I said, "I think maybe the *thing* is a little cuter." He grinned like I'd paid him a major compliment, and it seemed like we all let out our breath at the same time.

Jason's disgusting shark had taken some of the tension away, but I still felt unsafe. At any moment someone might say something about my father, and I'd float away like a feather.

Karl said, "Jennie, do you and Molly have any plans?"

I stared at my mother hopefully.

"We're setting out in the morning for the Virgin Islands," she said softly.

"*Tomorrow* morning?" Elizabeth cried. Her father frowned at her. She slid closer to me on the seat.

My mother sighed. "I want to leave before this depression worsens. We're putting the boat up for sale there." The boat. She never called it *Emerald Eyes* anymore.

Everyone was quiet.

Then Karl said, "Of course, of course, you must do what's best."

"We understand," Gina said. "I'd sell our boat right away if anything happened to Karl." Her eyes got dreamy. "It might be nice to have a little house again." She stopped and her cheeks flushed. Karl lifted his eyebrows at her. Gina made it worse by trying to explain herself.

Elizabeth rolled her eyes. "We know what you meant, Mom."

"What about *your* plans?" my mother asked.

"We're on our way to Venezuela," Karl said. "We'll leave as soon as this depression makes up its mind."

"Please, Mom," I said. "Couldn't we go with them?"

She stared at Elizabeth and me. I thought she might say yes. But she pressed her lips together and shook her head.

44

Elizabeth touched her pinkie to mine.

Karl jumped up and clapped his hands. "Here's Roger," he said. He gave my shoulder a squeeze as he went to greet him.

I didn't leave my seat during the cheery reunion. Roger invited everyone to his boat for the weather update.

"No thanks," I snapped.

"Molly . . . " my mother warned.

Elizabeth looked surprised. She had never seen my mother and me at odds—she didn't even know about my father's drinking—but she knew I needed support. Quickly she said, "Molly invited me over to *Emerald Eyes.* We haven't seen each other in months."

"Can I come, too?" Jason cried.

Elizabeth said, "Absolutely not." But I agreed, surprising her and myself. I'd wanted so much to be with her, to tell her about my plans. Now I was afraid to be alone with her, afraid she'd bring up my father.

On *Emerald Eyes,* Jason became more and more forlorn and I knew I'd made a mistake allowing him to join us. He pointed to the hook embedded in a teak beam overhead. "Where's Peety?" he asked. Out of the corner of my eye, I saw Elizabeth lower her head. Everything felt so different between us. So wrong.

"I put him away."

"How come?"

Exasperated, Elizabeth tugged on his sleeve. Jason wandered away, then peeked into my cabin. He turned and stared at me. I knew he'd seen Peety against my pillow.

Watching him trudge up the stairs, his shoulders drooping, I remembered the times my father had taken him fishing, how they'd pretend to return empty-handed, only to whip out a fat grouper. I remembered hearing their dumb jokes and watching Jason hang around my father like a puppy underfoot. The last time we were all together, Jason announced he was going to be a detective when he grew up. A detective just like my father.

We were quiet as I motored them back to *Magic*. When I pulled alongside, Jason almost knocked Elizabeth overboard when he sprang from the dinghy and disappeared below. Before I could push off, he rushed back on deck, his ears poking through his hair like pink clam shells. Then he handed me the scarlet feather with the black tip. I couldn't find the voice to say "thank you," but he must have seen it in my eyes.

I drifted away from *Magic*, the feather tight against my chest. Knowing I'd soon be leaving Elizabeth—and Jason—forever. Knowing I might not have enough time to save *Emerald Eyes*.

Six

A PALE MOON LINGERED IN THE DAWN SKY and drifted by my open hatch as the boat swung on its anchor. The sheet had wrapped around my feet during a bad dream about my father. Peety rested in the crook of my arm. The nightmare left a feeling of emptiness inside me, emptiness rapidly filling with shame. It was the worst kind of nightmare because it had really happened. There was no way I could make it up to him—not unless I saved *Emerald Eyes*.

I had so little time and so much to do. But I knew what I had to do next.

Quietly I stole into the darkened cabin and pulled the lid off the ice box. The heavy cover slipped from my sweaty fingers. I held my breath. If the noise didn't wake my mother, I was sure she'd hear the beating of my heart, so loud in my ears. For the longest time I didn't move. Finally, I dug deep into the freezer compartment, took what I came for, and rushed back to my cabin.

I ripped the ice-cold plastic away and stared at the thick wad of money. Hundreds of dollars, hidden when we first set sail. Money for emergencies only. Tears filled my eyes. But why should I feel guilty? I thought. It wasn't really stealing; it was my money, too. My father would be the first to say so. And surely there was no greater emergency than this. I blinked my tears away. Some of the cruisers would be selling used boat supplies on the beach in the morning. I intended to be there.

I tried to sleep, but felt I was being watched like a criminal. I pulled the book from under my pillow, browsed through it, then slipped Jason's feather between the pages. On my chest, the book lifted and fell with my beating heart. Would I be as brave as Tania if I ran into gales? I heard waves slap against the hull, and I was seized by a new fear. Suppose *Emerald Eyes* started sinking while I was at sea? Did I know where all the through-hull fittings were? If one of the hoses broke lose from a fitting, water would pour into the boat and sink it. *I have to remember to check them,* I thought. Hugging Peety tightly, imagining the *slosh, slosh* of water on the cabin floor, I fell into a restless sleep.

My cabin smelled like coffee, so I knew my mother was already up. A man's voice startled me. What was Roger doing here so early in the morning? I hopped from my bunk, smacked open the door, and stormed into the main cabin.

Jason's laugh made me leap in the air. He sang, "Molly's in her underpants!"

"Jason!" I screeched, trying to stretch my T-shirt over my knees. "What are you doing down here?"

"Looking at you in your underwear!"

I slammed my cabin door and dressed quickly. He was still waiting when I came back out. I kept my nose in the air as I marched by him. In the cockpit Roger and my mother were going over a chart. Their shoulders were touching. Across from them, Karl was studying a guidebook.

My mother looked up at me and seemed to lean away from Roger. "Well, we won't be leaving for the Virgin Islands," she said. "We have a growing tropical storm on our hands." I bit my lip to keep from smiling.

"There's more bad news," Karl said, that jokey look in his eyes. "We're all going to the same island together."

Jason waved the shark bottle at me, an evil grin on his face. Before he could mention my underwear again, I shoved a piece of bran muffin in his mouth.

Roger laughed. "Hey, Moll, maybe this storm came along so you could have a good visit with *Magic*." He held a wedge of pineapple out, and it smelled so sweet, looked so juicy, it was hard to resist. When I shook my head, he gave it to my mother.

Already the storm winds were gusting to fifty-five miles per hour and were expected to strengthen. But I was sure there was nothing to worry about. In my heart I believed the storm was another gift from my father, a gift of time to help me save *Emerald Eyes*.

"It's too soon to know what track the storm will take," my mother said, "or how bad it might get. It could go north or south of us, but rather than take a chance, we're sailing to Manchioneel Island. You remember Hurricane Lagoon, Molly? We anchored there the last time we sailed to Manchioneel. If worse comes to worst, we can tie into the mangroves there during the storm. After we clear customs this morning, we'll all leave for Aves Island, spend the night there, then head for Manchioneel tomorrow." A change had come over my mother. Her confusion, the hesitancy, were gone. Instead of frightening her more, the threat of a potential hurricane had mobilized her into action.

"Since we're not going back to St. Thomas, can we sail to Venezuela afterwards?" I asked.

My mother's eyes wavered. "We'll see. Let's deal with things as they come."

Karl said, "A friend of yours is very upset about this change of plans." He tossed his head toward *Magic*.

I looked over at Elizabeth. She punched the air with her fists and did a little jig for me. This time I couldn't keep the smile off my face. I nodded when she held up a book to show me she still had school work to finish. My mother didn't say anything about my school work. I'd spent so much time reading *Maiden Voyage* and making notes, I guess she thought I was studying like crazy.

After everyone was gone, I mentioned the beach sale.

"We need to get rid of junk," she said, "not buy more."

"Can I go over?"

"We don't need—"

"They might have some good books! Can't I just look?"

"Okay. I'll call Roger and ask him to pick me up on the way to Customs."

Marine supplies were spread out on blankets along the beach, a lot of it junk, just like Mom said. But I managed to find two charts I might need, and one cruiser had a used GPS for sale.

"Are you sure it works?" I asked, pressing buttons. The GPS, a Global Positioning System, was a navigation aid, but unlike the stationary one in our main cabin, this one was handheld. I didn't want to go below every time I had to check our latitude and longitude or get a new course heading, but mainly I wanted it because I sometimes got seasick in the cabin during rough weather. Besides there might be times when I couldn't leave the helm. And what if our GPS stopped working? I needed a spare. My parents knew celestial navigation, using the sun and stars, but I still hadn't learned. Sailing alone would be nothing like sailing with a family.

The man said, "Aren't you the girl on *Emerald Eyes*? Tell your mother to stop by—"

"No, no. See, it's . . . a . . . a birthday present for her. Our last one broke. Don't tell her, okay?"

"It works fine—it's almost new. But maybe you should buy your mother something else. She might not want this brand—"

"Molly!"

I spun around. Elizabeth was walking out of the water.

"I'll take it. I'll take it," I whispered. "This is the *exact* kind she wants." My hand shook as I handed him the money, more money than I'd ever spent before. Quickly I stuffed the instrument in my bag.

Elizabeth ran up, water running down her freckles. "Hi."

"Hi," I answered, happy to see her.

"What'd you buy?"

"Nothing," I answered guiltily. "You cut your hair," I said. Why am I talking about *hair*? I couldn't believe how nervous I was.

"Yeah. I put goo in it to make it spikey, but it keeps drooping down from the salt air."

"I like your little beaded braids."

"I was thinking of beading my whole head, but decided on just a few braids for my bangs. I bought you some beads, too."

Then we spoke at the same time: I said, "There's something I have to tell—" as she said "—I didn't want to be the only one looking weird."

A voice chirped behind us. "Don't worry, you're both weird."

Elizabeth yelled, "Jason, stop following us!"

"I'm not! I'm just going in the same direction. Dad told me to wait for him. He left your stuff over there."

"I'm sorry, Molly. What were you going to tell me?"

"Later," I whispered, tossing my head toward Jason. Her eyes lit up.

We followed him to a table under the awning of the outdoor restaurant. Around his neck he wore the bottle with the shriveled shark. I kept my back to the shark pool, but got a chill anyway just thinking about my last conversation with Daddy.

"That thing is disgusting, Jason. How could you wear it?" I said.

"Don't tell him that," Elizabeth warned. "He'll never take it off. Besides, it's his only friend."

"Very funny," he said. "At least it's not a girl."

"Give me your foot," Elizabeth said to me.

"Why?"

She plunked it in her lap. "Close your eyes . . . . Keep them shut!" I felt her fingers on my ankle. "Okay," she said finally. When I opened my eyes, I was wearing a thin silver ankle bracelet with my name etched in the center of a small heart.

"Happy belated birthday," Elizabeth announced.

"I love it, Elizabeth." I held my leg out, turning my foot back and forth. Then I hugged her.

"Yuck!" Jason cried.

"There's more to the present," she said, pulling a roll of toilet paper out of her bag. She grabbed my foot again.

"Toilet paper?" Jason said. "Gross present!"

"Watch I don't wrap you in toilet paper, Jason—and flush you." Elizabeth twisted some toilet paper into a long coil and wove it through my toes to separate them. She lined up different bottles of nail polish and opened each one. Her own toenails were painted different colors.

I heard laughter behind me and knew it was Christopher before Elizabeth spoke. "Don't turn around," she whispered. "It's a really cute guy."

"Watch it!" I said. "You got purple polish on my toe."

"I think he's in love with me already," she said. "Don't worry, there's an ugly guy with him who's perfect for you."

"Hey, Molly! How you doing?" Christopher called to my back. I stuffed the roll of toilet paper into the bag with the GPS and my money.

Elizabeth puffed her cheeks out like a blow fish. "That was the ugly one calling you. Trust me."

"They're both ugly," Jason said. "If they fall in, they'll make the sharks puke." Elizabeth reached to swat his bottom, but he ducked away.

"Now you got polish on my knee," I whined.

"I'm glad I didn't waste my string bikini on that cute one," she said, peering over my shoulder. "He hasn't taken his eyes off you."

"You have a *string* bikini?"

"Over my father's dead body." She gasped in horror. "I'm sorry, Molly," she moaned, rubbing my knee briskly with polish remover.

I moved my knee before she rubbed the skin off. "It's okay," I said, avoiding her eyes.

Listening to Christopher horse around by the sharks made my stomach flutter uncomfortably. The memory of my secret glided past like a dark shadow. Unable to resist, I turned.

He was balanced on one leg, making jokes about the sharks with his beer-belly friend. Acting like a drunken tightrope walker, he hopped across the walkway on one foot and came toward us. I was wearing shorts, but hugged my arms, wishing I had a shirt to cover my bathing suit top.

He was still laughing when he reached us. "Hi, Molly."

I swung my feet under the table to hide the toilet paper between my toes. He fanned his hand in a wave as I introduced Elizabeth and Jason. The other guy snapped his fingers twice to hurry Christopher. Frowning, Jason watched him intently.

"Hey, Turner," Christopher said. "We have a few minutes. What's the hurry?" The man ignored him and kept walking.

"I know that guy," Jason said. "Doesn't he have a black boat?"

"Yup. I'm his new first mate."

"He's a jerk."

"JASON!" Elizabeth and I shouted at the same time.

"Well, he is."

Christopher was grinning. "I've got a little brother just like you. Come on, I want to introduce you to a hungry shark."

"How about this shark?" Jason said, waving the bottle around his neck.

Christopher studied the bottle. "Not bad, not bad, but a little shrimpy. I've got a great white shark in a bottle. I don't wear him much cause he weighs a thousand pounds and gives me a pain in the neck . . . like you." Jason's face yanked up in a grin and Christopher ruffled his hair.

"There's a hurricane coming," Jason said.

Turner walked toward us. "Gimme a break. It's only a storm, and it'll veer away by tomorrow."

Christopher nodded. "It'll turn north. Turner says they all do."

"Let's move it, Chris. I want to sail out of here."

"Where you sailing to?" Jason asked.

"You writing a book?" Turner asked sharply.

Christopher's face was expressionless. "We're meeting up with some friends," he said. "Gotta go." He backed away, smiling at me.

"How could someone so cute, hang out with such a creep?" Elizabeth said after they left.

"He's a jail bird," Jason replied.

"What? Who's a jail bird?" I asked.

Elizabeth took his ear between her fingers. "Who? Tell us," she demanded.

"Let go! The fat guy."

"Don't spread rumors like that," Elizabeth scolded. "Who said he was in jail?"

Jason slumped in a chair and tried to tuck his ears under his hair. "I heard it once. It was for smuggling or something. And you can't teach an old leopard new tricks."

"Jason, sometimes you worry me," I said. "I think the sun is doing something spooky to your brain."

Grinning, he grabbed for my bag, and I snatched it back from his hands.

"I just want to see what you bought before."

"I didn't buy anything," I snapped.

"Liar, liar, pants on fire. I saw you buy something. It was either the cell phone or the GPS that guy had."

My face burned. "It's . . . it's the GPS, Jason, but it's a

secret, okay. It's for my mother. Her birthday's coming up."

"Don't worry, I won't tell," he said. He was a pain in the neck, but I knew I could trust him about something like that.

Christopher turned at the dock and waved. I never heard my mother walk up. Suddenly she was beside me. I could feel the warning energy radiating from her body and thought she'd overheard me tell Jason about the GPS. Then I saw the guarded look on her face, a look that first appeared when Daddy began to drink. She was watching Christopher the way she used to watch my father when she thought I needed her protection.

Roger walked up. "I know you already shopped," he said, holding out a paper bag. "But they had some really nice mangoes, so I got you some. I remembered how much you liked them."

Did he also remember how much my father liked them? How we'd eat them in our bathing suits, then dive overboard to wash the juice off? My mother smiled at him when she took the bag. Her fingers brushed his.

Impulsively I jumped up and shouted to Christopher. "Hope I see you again! We're going to Manchioneel!" Feeling foolish, I plopped down quickly and hid my toilet-papered toes under the table. *Why did I do that?* I wondered. It was Elizabeth I wanted to be with, not Christopher. At that point, I didn't really care if I saw him again. It was only later that I came to care. And by then it was too late, for both of us.

Elizabeth was staring at me with the strangest look on her face. I thought it was because of Christopher. Instead, she leaned close and whispered, "Your mother's birthday was two months ago, Molly. What's going on?"

Seven

"**Y**OU'RE DOING WHAT?" Elizabeth shouted.

"Shhh," I hissed. "Would you keep your voice down? I'm taking *Emerald Eyes*."

"You're stealing the boat?"

"How can I steal it when it's mine?"

We had to stop talking when her father approached after clearing out with Customs and Immigration. Walking to the dinghy, we hung back, but only had a moment.

Elizabeth gripped my arm. "Molly, I swear, if you do anything without talking to me first, I'll . . . I'll never talk to you again."

"Promise you'll help me?" I asked. Her eyes shone. "Well?"

She still hadn't answered me when her father called from the dinghy.

Later, I found my mother with her head in her hands at the table in the cabin. She looked up and her face was streaked with tears.

"Your father took our emergency money," she said. Her words sizzled in the air. "All of it. It's gone."

I squeezed my hands into fists to stop their shaking. "How do you know it was him?" I stammered.

She slammed the flat of her hand against the table. "Stop defending his actions! Who else took it? You? He must have done it when he was drunk. Oh, God—" She clasped her hand over her mouth to keep from crying.

I backed away. I couldn't stand to see the hurt in her eyes. I couldn't stand myself. *I'm sorry, Daddy,* I thought. It didn't seem like enough. But there was no way to right the wrong. Not without telling the truth.

In silence my mother and I prepared *Emerald Eyes* for the sail to Aves. The thought of setting out without my father for the first time gave me a lopsided feeling, like a wounded bird trying to fly on one wing.

My mother had spent her whole life sailing on Long Island's Great South Bay. She had even taught my father to sail. Before he met her, he only drove speed boats.

"The first time your Mom took me sailing, I ran us aground on an outgoing tide. We were stuck there alone for five hours." He wiggles his eyebrows at Mom and gives her his extra-watt smile. *"Smartest move I ever made."*

We each had our own assignments for getting the boat ready. I ran my thumb over the heavy bronze ports that we let turn a deep natural green. I screwed the ports shut, making them watertight in case the rail went under while we sailed. Before going on deck, I stored everything in the cabin so stuff wouldn't crash around if we heeled.

At the bow, I pulled on the bottom of the sailbag. The jib spilled out like a pile of fresh white sheets from a dryer. Our cutter-rigged sloop had one tall mast for the mainsail, plus two headsails, a staysail on a small boom in front of the mast, and another headsail at the bow.

I remembered the hours I'd spent—the frustration—learning to tie a bowline knot. Every time I thought I had it, my fingers would tangle in the rope. Now it felt as natural as breathing. I tied two long lines called jib sheets to the sail with bowlines, fed the lines through the leads, and brought them back to the cockpit so we could trim the sail when we were underway.

Mom came on deck and looked around. I think we both noticed at the same time that the mainsail cover was still on, one of my father's jobs. Mom's shoulders sagged. She moved toward the boom, but I stepped ahead of her. Roughly I tore at the hooks and yanked the green cover off. I might as well do my father's jobs. Soon I'd be doing everything myself anyway.

From below, we heard Roger's voice calling us on the VHF radio. My mother went down to answer.

The engine was already on, and I stormed to the bow to weigh anchor. The electric winch brought our chain up feeding it into the well, and I only needed to lift the anchor, a 45-pound Danforth, a few feet by hand. My mother called, "Wait, Molly! I'll be right there!" A barnacle bit into my hand and a blossom of blood appeared as I struggled with the anchor.

"Why didn't you wait for me?" she asked as I returned to the helm.

I slipped my hand in my pocket to hide the blood.

"What if something happened to you? Shouldn't I know how to handle the boat alone?"

"You're not alone! We'll help each other."

I turned the wheel toward *Magic*, passing Roger on *Golden Slippers*, still hauling up his anchor.

I pretended to stare at the instrument panel when he waved.

Elizabeth was also at the helm, Jason beside her, while their parents finished other chores. Side by side, we motored toward the harbor entrance. *Magic* weaved back and forth as Jason tried to wrestle the helm from Elizabeth. Karl finally stuck his hands on his hips in warning.

"How about we get some sail up?" Mom said.

"I'll do it." I had hoped to do everything alone—a trial run for my maiden voyage.

"*We'll* do it," she answered firmly, walking to the mast.

I brought the boat around, watching the burgee on the starboard shroud until it fluttered fore and aft, showing that we were pointing directly into the wind. The flapping main and staysail sounded like a flock of large birds as Mom hoisted them to the top of the mast. Then she hauled up the headsail, which unfolded from the bow like a big helium balloon. We trimmed the sails together from the cockpit, my mother cranking the winch while I tailed the line to take up the slack. I couldn't stop her from helping me, but I knew I didn't need her.

The wind lifted *Emerald Eyes* and she built up speed, heeling slightly as we headed from the harbor. Elizabeth steered off the wind, and our boats moved apart. I sailed as close to the wind as possible without luffing, never easing off, never giving an inch.

I let go of the wheel for a moment, and we balanced

perfectly on the wind, as if the boat knew where she needed to go.

"I'll give you the heading," Mom said.

"I know it," I answered, looking at the compass. "I charted the course myself." My mother's eyebrows lifted in surprise, and I was sorry I'd told her.

Over my shoulder, I watched the island grow smaller, wishing there was a way to sail back in time. Beyond us a sailboat looked like an angel flying from Calabash Bay.

Five hours later, we approached Aves Island. It was tourist season when we sailed there last, with so many masts it looked like a magical forest in the middle of a sea-blue desert. Now, like my father, the forest was gone.

During the sail, I'd watched for dolphins. As we rounded the reef, I thought I finally saw one, but it was only a piece of driftwood. Daddy loved it when dolphins frolicked around the boat, crossing our bow, zigging through our wake. *"They're good luck, McGoo. They'll save us if we ever get in trouble. Dolphins are Irish, you know."* For the first time ever, not one dolphin joined *Emerald Eyes*. Had the dolphins abandoned me? I shook off a sense of foreboding. My father would never let anything happen to *Emerald Eyes*. He would never let anything happen to me.

On the south side of the island, I steered toward a ribbon of sandy beach lined with coconut palms. I wanted to anchor the boat alone, but I was afraid my mother would become suspicious. From the bow, she watched the bottom intently, then raised her hand, the signal to stop. I reversed the engine, stopping the boat's forward motion, and kept it in reverse while the chain rumbled from its well, *chunk, chunk, chunk.* When the anchor bit into the patch of sand my mother had chosen, the bow swung around. I gave a burst of power to make certain the anchor was set.

"Looks like we might get some rain, Molly. Let's get the raincatcher up." Water had been brackish at Calabash, so we hadn't filled the tank. If it didn't rain soon, we could run out of fresh water. My heart started racing. What if I ran out of water crossing the ocean? I tried to remember if that had ever happened to Tania. I eyed the four water jugs that were tied along the rail. *Don't forget to fill them, as well as the tank, before you sail away*, I thought.

We stretched our water catcher, a heavy piece of canvas, across the deck and tied it to the shrouds to keep it aloft. One end of a hose was attached to a spigot in the canvas, and I inserted the other end into the fill hole in the deck, so the rain would drain into our tank below.

Blowing toward us, the rain looked like a silk curtain floating in a light breeze. It drifted across the boat, barely wetting the decks, but behind it a dark gray wall closed rapidly. When it hit, the rain pounded the decks, and Mom got caught in the downpour.

She looked like a wet shaggy dog, her hair flattened across her head, covering her eyes. I threw a towel to her and she rubbed the wet hair back from her eyes and dried her arms, which were covered in little goose bumps.

The raincatcher was heavy with water, and I went below to listen to it fill our tank. The heavy rain was so loud at first, I had to turn my ear toward the floorboards. I heard the beat of the steel drums as rain poured into the stainless-steel water tank. *Fill 'er up baby! Listen to those Calypso drums. Nature's jamming in the bilge, McGoo.* I stared up at Mom. Her smile vanished when she saw the look on my face.

By late afternoon Hank was a hurricane.

Feeding on the warm sea, it was growing in size and

intensity, but the weather service was still unsure about its projected path. The hurricane was wobbling instead of moving forward, as if it couldn't decide whether to come for us. If it veered north or south, it would miss us. If it went due west, we could be directly in its path. Still, I never worried. The longer the storm took to make up its mind, the more time I had to figure things out.

I heard Elizabeth shout from the water. "Jason! Watch your flippers! You almost killed me!" She swam away from him as a spray of spit burst from his snorkel.

"You doing school work, Molly?" She pulled her mask up.

"Be right in," I said, stuffing my notebook out of sight. Actually, I had done some school work for the first time. A new thought popped into my mind and worried me. If I continued with correspondence school when I left with *Emerald Eyes*, my mother would be able to track me down. I wasn't crazy about school, but the thought of being a drop-out upset me. I hoped Elizabeth would have some ideas.

Roger was swimming over, too. Briefly I watched him. If I squinted my eyes just right, he could have been my father. I yanked on my yellow flippers. When he grabbed onto our ladder, I leaped in the water over his head, and I didn't look back when he called my name.

Elizabeth and I waddled ashore like clumsy giant birds and left our masks and fins against a palm tree. Jason ran ahead, tossing chunks of dead coral into the trees, trying to knock down the coconuts. I watched Roger at the helm of our boat, resting his folded arms across my father's wheel.

Elizabeth followed my eyes. "What's wrong?"

"Nothing," I said. I was too ashamed of my mother to tell Elizabeth about her and Roger.

Elizabeth jammed her fists on her waist. "Okay," she said, "let's make sure I got this straight. You're running away from home . . . . I mean, you're running away with your home?"

"It's not funny, Elizabeth."

"Who's laughing?" She waited a moment, then said, "You're serious."

I nodded.

"Okay, that's it!" She threw her hands in the air. The beads bounced in her short hair. "My friend has had a nervous breakdown. She has completely lost her mind. She needs a rest, that's all, then she'll be normal again. Well, almost normal." She looked at my face, then gripped my wrist. "You're scaring me. Smile or something."

Jason called from the other end of the beach and held up a coconut. She dragged me under a tamarind tree. Sitting, I dug my heels into the cool sand, and she squeezed my big toes, one silver, the other gold.

"Don't get mad," she said. "But you can't sail *Emerald Eyes* yourself. That's crazy."

"I can! I know how to sail. I know how to navigate. I can do it."

"No, you can't do it."

"I thought you'd help me!" I turned to hide my face.

"Oh, Molly, don't cry. I'm sorry."

"I'm not crying!" I dug my fingernails into my palms to make my eyes stop tearing.

"Okay, okay, you're not crying. I know how upset you are, really. Your father . . . oh gosh, he was the best, I swear." Her nose turned red, her eyes brimming with tears. "I know how much you loved him. I loved him and he wasn't even my father. But he'd never want you to do this. He'd never want you to sail away by yourself."

"He gave me *Maiden Voyage*! For my last birthday."

"So?"

"So? Don't you see? Tania Aebi? The youngest girl to sail around the world alone? It was his last gift to me. Like he knew. Like he wanted me to do this."

Elizabeth was shaking her head. "No, you're reading into it. He gave you the book. It was a present. Period. I have the same book. That's probably where he got the idea. He did not give it to you because he knew he was going to . . . because he knew anything. Don't do this, Molly."

"I thought you were my friend."

"I *am* your friend. Your best friend."

"Well, you're not acting like one." I jumped up and ran to the shore. Elizabeth followed. My new ankle bracelet glistened under water.

As we walked through the surf, she took my hand. "Let's be logical, Moll." I tried to pull my hand away, but she wouldn't release it. "First of all, you are *not* Tania. She was the youngest to complete a solo circumnavigation. But she wasn't a girl—she was a *woman*. She was *eighteen* when she started, a lot older than you."

"Four years, big deal."

"A very big deal. Furthermore, she was not sailing a forty-foot boat. I bet *Emerald Eyes* is at least fifteen feet bigger than her boat."

I kicked at the water.

"You don't even have roller furling, Molly. I know, I know, neither did she—but suppose you have to walk out on deck to drag your sails down?"

"I can do that easily."

"Sure, when it's calm. Try it in a monster storm with

humongous waves! Try it in the middle of the night. Your sails are much bigger and heavier than hers. You'd be washed overboard." I got a sinking feeling in my stomach. Did Elizabeth know how my father died?

"A million things could go wrong," she insisted. "Suppose you have to go up the mast? If you lose a halyard at the top, you'd be floating around in the middle of the ocean with no way to raise the sail."

"I have that figured out, but I'll need you to help—"

"And there's another thing, Molly. Tania wasn't running away. Her father wanted her to go."

"So does mine!"

"He does not! You'd have to hide out from your mother. You'd have to hide from everyone. Tania wasn't in hiding. People helped her. She even met cute *guys* who helped her!"

We stared at each other.

"Okay, that's *one* good thing about your idea—but it's the only good thing. Suppose you needed repairs to the boat, Molly? How much money do you have?"

"Enough."

"You do not. And where did you get the money for that GPS? Even used, it must have cost a lot."

Too ashamed to tell her the truth, I looked away. "It was birthday money from my grandmother."

"Well, you couldn't have much left."

"I can make money," I said.

"How?"

"I don't know! I can clean boat bottoms."

"And get those tiny shrimps in your hair and up your nose? They'll start breeding in your sinuses—"

"Will you stop!"

"Tania wrote magazine articles about her adventure to

earn money. You can't do that if you're hiding your identity."

She held both my hands and looked into my eyes. "You'll be all alone, Molly. Even Tania wasn't alone. She had a cat."

"I'm allergic to cats."

Elizabeth grinned sarcastically. "I rest my case."

"I can't let my mother sell the boat," I said, shaking my hands free.

"Well, you can't take the boat alone," she answered. "It's too much for one person."

The sound of Jason's screams sent ice water through my veins. The blood drained from Elizabeth's face. Together we raced along the beach. The wet sand was hard under our pounding bare feet. Rounding the bend, we almost knocked him down. He was leaping around, hollering at the top of his lungs. A hermit crab with big red pincers, still in a borrowed shell, had a tight grip on one of his fingers.

Elizabeth hugged him. I guess she was overcome with relief that he wasn't being eaten by sharks or barracudas. He wriggled out of her grip. "Let go! You're making me puke!"

She took his wrist and gently pulled on the shell. The crab claws tightened. Jason howled. I suppose she felt stupid for slobbering all over him and tried to make a joke. "I think if we pour kerosene on your hand and light it, the thing will let go."

"Very funny! It hurts."

I grabbed his hand and ripped the crab free. Jason wailed. I held out the hermit crab. "Do you want to put this in your pocket as a souvenir?" He gave me a dirty look.

I wanted to say more to Elizabeth, but we couldn't talk in front of Jason. I stared out at *Emerald Eyes*, and Elizabeth followed my gaze. Roger and my mother were going below together. Sudden tears stung my eyes.

"Molly?" Elizabeth whispered. "What is it? Are you upset because you can't sail away by yourself?"

I clenched my fists and made my decision: If the boat was too big for me to sail alone, I'd find someone to help me. One way or another, I'd keep my mother from selling *Emerald Eyes*.

Jason's eyes widened. "Hey, it's that guy, Christopher!"

Even before I turned, I felt like I was balanced on the precipice of a rogue wave, about to careen down the other side, out of control.

Eight

"SHARKS!" Jason shouted.

I whirled. In the distance Christopher was in water up to his waist, water the color of blood.

"Would you quit it?" Elizabeth scolded. She hooked her arm around her brother's neck in a strangle-hold, dragging him with us.

Christopher was helping a man and woman rinse a red cotton blanket in the water, red dye bleeding into the clear surf. Holding the blanket up, dye ran into the armpits of his shirt and it looked as if he'd sweated blood.

The stained water curled around his waist as though blood were draining from his body. A chill of foreboding made me shiver and step back when the blood-red sea crept toward my feet.

I thought Christopher sounded annoyed when he spotted us. "What are you doing here? You said you were going to Manchioneel."

"We are," I answered defensively. "But we're spending the night here first."

I must have mistaken his surprise for annoyance, because he smiled quickly like he was really glad to see us. "I was just giving these people a hand, Peter and Theresa."

It had seemed weird calling grown-ups by their first names when we first moved aboard *Emerald Eyes*. But cruising kids always did that. I guess because it was so hard to find other kids sometimes. And if we didn't make friends with grown-ups, we might not have any friends at all.

"I thought there was a shark attack," Jason complained, staring at the red water around Christopher's legs.

"You *wished* it was a shark attack," Christopher said, grabbing him. "You bring this little squirt everywhere you go?" he asked us.

"Too bad it *wasn't* a shark attack!" Jason taunted, splashing him. Christopher dived and surfaced like a whale behind Jason. "I've got something better than sharks for you," Christopher told him. "A bat attack!" He grabbed Jason's foot and pretended to bite it.

"I love bats," Jason said, grinning.

"Not *these* bats," Christopher said. "A guy I knew in Venezuela got bitten on the toe by a vampire bat while he was sleeping. Didn't feel it or notice the blood on his sheet, didn't even know it happened, 'til he got rabies and slobbered to death!" Elizabeth's face wrinkled in horror, and she stared at her feet through the water. Jason's face was one big grin when Christopher said, "I've got a bat with your name on it." Christopher hung onto Jason's toes when he tried to swim away.

Elizabeth and I escaped their splashing and helped

carry the blanket to a dinghy. "I don't know what I was thinking, buying a red blanket," Theresa said. "The stupid thing blew right over the side when I was airing it. That nice boy just stopped by to help." Elizabeth and I were leaning over with our backsides out so the dye wouldn't ruin our bathing suits. I peeked over my shoulder quickly, but Christopher was too busy teasing Jason to notice us.

"Thanks for helping, girls." Theresa wore lots of make-up, pink smudges on her cheeks and mascara that left a black snake running from one eye.

"Yeah, sure appreciate it," Peter said. "It's been one of those days." He was completely bald on top, but a wispy, white fringe grew around the back of his head. His skin was pink, except for his nose, which was very red and peeling.

Elizabeth called to Jason, who was swimming out too far, and he splashed toward us, his giggles making the woman smile. Christopher dog-paddled behind Jason, humming the theme from *Jaws*. Laughing, Jason staggered toward Elizabeth and knocked her in the water. She muttered a nasty word under her breath.

Jason grinned and wagged his finger. "I'm telling on you for saying that. You're going to get in trouble."

"Where are you kids anchored?" Peter asked.

"Right around that bend." I pointed to the far end of the beach.

"And that must be your little brother," he said to me.

"Oh, *puleeze*!" I cried.

"We don't know who he is," Elizabeth said in a serious voice. "We think he's an illegal alien. Not from another country, from another *planet*."

Christopher waded from the water. He pushed his wet hair back with both hands and smiled at me. Beads of water ran down his face.

"We didn't see your boat," I said to him.

He frowned briefly then shrugged. "It's anchored in the other cove."

I'd always thought the only other cove had very poor holding ground. "How come you're not anchored out here or around the spit by us?" I asked.

A hidden thought seemed to skitter through his eyes like a bat. "We like privacy," he answered.

"Where's your boat?" Jason asked Peter.

The man pointed to a beautiful yacht off the beach. "That's us on *Dreamer*."

"*That's your boat?* Man, I'd love a boat like that," Christopher said.

"Well, she might be for sale soon," Peter answered. "I think the wife is about ready for that condominium."

Theresa stuck her hands on her wide hips. "The *wife* has been ready for a long time." I could tell she wasn't really mad.

"I might be interested," Christopher said. "What do you want for it?" The boat looked pretty expensive and I wondered how Christopher could afford it. Even Peter smiled a little. When he heard the price, Christopher's shoulders slumped. He stared at *Dreamer* like a little boy without a ticket outside a circus tent.

"How many does she sleep?" Christopher asked.

"She's got three state rooms," Peter answered.

Jason yelled, "There's my father!" We waved our arms until Karl spotted us. Christopher was standing apart, still staring at *Dreamer*.

"I got attacked by a crab, Dad," Jason cried when Karl pulled up. "And we almost got to see a shark attack. And a bat bit someone on the toe, and he got rabies 'cause he didn't know."

Karl had an amused look on his face. Elizabeth wiggled her toes nervously.

"Time for dinner, kids. Your mother is worried about you, Molly."

I mentioned the snorkeling equipment, and Christopher spoke up quickly. "I'll take you to get it, Molly."

"We can get it ourselves." Elizabeth's voice was frosty.

"I left something on the beach," he said. "I have to go back anyway, so I might as well take Molly." Watching his face, I remembered what a good liar he was.

He pushed the dinghy into deeper water, so his prop wouldn't touch bottom when he lowered it. He put his hands around my waist to boost me into his dinghy. "That's okay," I said, flustered. "I can get in myself." I was sure I looked like a whale as I lumbered over the inflated pontoon. My hair came unpinned and fell over my face.

He'd removed his stained shirt, and the muscles on his arms rippled when he started the motor. He grinned while I tried to pin my hair up again. "You look great. Your bathing suit matches your eyes." I hugged myself and pressed my knees together.

Karl said, "Don't forget to stop at *Emerald Eyes* first, Molly."

"Are you still coming for dinner?" Elizabeth called.

I pretended not to hear over the sound of the engine.

"Alone at last," he said, laughing, as we pulled away. I peeked over my shoulder at Elizabeth, disappointment and confusion on her face. Oddly, I felt the same way. We had so little time together. Why was I wasting it with a boy I hardly knew?

"Oh, man," Christopher said as we passed by *Dreamer*.

"Now *this* is a boat!" *Dreamer* was at least sixty-feet long, white and sleek, with roller furling on the jib and the mainsail. The varnished rails gleamed.

We circled twice, Christopher admiring every inch of the boat.

Mom's eyes were practically burning a hole through Christopher when we motored up. Roger was on board, which made me glad that Christopher was with me.

"Aren't you on *Sinbad?*" Roger asked. "How'd you get that damage on the hull?"

Christopher laughed. "Man, we were almost wiped out by a freighter in the middle of the night."

"What happened?" my mother asked in a tight voice.

"I was sleeping and heard this major crunch. When I looked up, this giant freighter was practically on top of us. Didn't even stop. Just kept going."

"Was someone on watch?" My mother's voice shook with controlled anger. Even Roger could tell and looked away.

"Nah. We were both asleep. You know how it is."

Mom definitely did *not* know how it was. It was a rule that one of us was always awake on *Emerald Eyes.* A hard smile bent the corners of my mouth. Single-handers like Tania—and me—*couldn't* be on watch all the time.

"We have to go back to the beach for the snorkeling gear," I said.

"I thought you were eating on *Magic.* You can get your stuff later." I noticed the barbecue on the stern rail, the hose attached to the propane tank. Roger was eating over. Just the two of them. What else did they have in mind besides dinner?

"I'm going over to *Magic* as soon as I pick up the snorkeling gear," I said. It wasn't a lie exactly. I had no idea what I was going to do.

When we pulled the dinghy up to the beach and loaded the gear into it, Christopher said, "Let's go for a walk."

We splashed through the surf without speaking, then headed toward some trees and sat down.

"I don't think your mother likes me," Christopher said. "But your father seems like a nice guy."

"He's *not* my father!"

"Wow, I must have hit a nerve. I just assumed that's all. Where's your old man?"

I didn't answer at first. Finally, and very softly, I said, "He's away."

"Is he meeting you someplace?"

"Yes." My voice sounded like a stranger's. "He's waiting for us at Manchioneel Island."

"Molly McGuire," Christopher said, sliding his fingers down my beaded braid. "You look like a Molly." I stared at the water, remembering how my father thought so, too.

"You were a little charmer, Molly, with that cute mop of red hair and those big eyes." Daddy tugs on one of the curls falling in my face.

"That *Dreamer* was something, wasn't it?" Christopher said. "I'm going to buy a boat like that. Then I'll get my little brother and sisters and sail them around the world. Man, they'd love it."

"How could you afford to buy a boat like *Dreamer?*"

The light changed his blue eyes to the color of rain. Behind his head, a gecko jumped on a leaf and changed its color to hide. "Well, I can't now. But some day. I've got some money coming in. I'll start saving."

"You'd have to save an awful lot."

He shrugged. "I'll manage, don't worry about that." He sat straight and juggled hard green sea grapes, then smacked them toward the water. "You an only child?"

"Thank goodness," I said, thinking of Jason.

"I walked out on my brother and sisters," he said. "Just left them. It was too much with me and my old man. I took a job crewing on a boat that was coming down to the islands. Hooked up with Turner recently. I'd sure like my own boat though. Get my brother and sisters out of that house. Take them cruising around the world. You use some correspondence school right?" I nodded. "Yeah, I could set that up for them. I'd be their teacher. Make them call me Professor Brother."

He leaned back on his elbows. "You get along with your parents?" he asked.

I nodded and cracked open a brittle tamarind. The sticky fruit tasted tart.

"You're lucky. My father disappears on these drunken binges every few months."

I spit out a flat seed. On the white sand, it looked like a dead beetle.

"It's not so bad when he's gone, you know, with just my mother. Every time he comes back though, he takes off after me. Says I'm not taking care of the family the way I'm supposed to." He snapped his arm out and tossed some leaves he'd crushed, but they floated down and landed in my lap. I picked them up and bounced them in my palm.

"It isn't your job to take care of the family," I said. He looked like a hurt little boy, and I wanted to reach out and put my finger on his chipped tooth. Fix it the way his parents should have.

"Yeah, I know. But the kids . . . I was angry and just took

off. My brother is eight, my sisters are nine and ten. Little guys. At least before, they had a big brother. Now they've got no one." He turned to me. "Do either of your parents drink?"

I shook my head.

He was quiet for a while. "He used to hit my mother. I should have stayed to protect her."

I leaned my chin on my knees and wished I'd brought my dark glasses. I never felt like I needed to protect my mother when Daddy was drinking. It was more like I had to protect my father against himself. Only I let him down in the end. The one time he really needed me. I jumped up and ran along the beach.

Christopher caught up with me and took my hand to slow me down. A tingly feeling ran through me. He released my hand when I reached up to fix my hair.

"Sorry, I shouldn't have bored you with all my problems. It's just so good having someone to talk to."

"No, I'm glad you told me. I felt like getting up, that's all. Can't you go home again?"

"Not a chance. But someday I'm going to buy a fancy yacht like *Dreamer*, and I'll mail my father a picture of it. Show him what a real success looks like. And then I'll get my brother and sisters out of there."

I imagined the photograph he'd send his father: He was standing on *Emerald Eyes*, standing right next to me. I blinked and folded my arms tightly across my chest.

"I'm never going back there. I'll die if I go back," he said. His dark hair fell forward across his eyes. I could see the uneven cut of his hair. I wanted to reach out and make it even. A breeze rattled the palms behind us, and sand blew across my feet.

"You watch. Someday soon I'll have a *real* boat. And I'll

sail around the world." He sounded like a child insisting he'll be a fireman when he grows up. Or a policeman. I looked away.

We walked in silence for awhile. Then he asked, "How old are you anyway?"

"Eighteen," I said. He grinned.

"Seventeen?" I tried.

"I figure . . . fifteen, *maybe* sixteen."

I nodded vigorously. "That's what I am, fifteen or sixteen. How old are you?"

Laughing, he said, "Older. Let's go. Turner's probably freaking out."

"Why would he care where you are?"

"Oh, we're doing something later." He walked toward the dinghy.

"He's kind of creepy, isn't he? How come you hang out with him?"

"Nah, he's okay. He helped me out when I needed a place to stay."

He was towing the dinghy into the water. I blurted my question to his back. "Was he ever in jail?"

Slowly, he turned. "Where'd you hear something like that?"

I shrugged. "I don't remember. He wasn't a smuggler was he?"

I could see him weighing his next words. He looked me in the eye. "You think I'd be mixed up with a guy like that?"

I wanted him to say more and waited.

"Okay, promise you won't repeat this to anyone. I heard the same thing about him. Some people have nothing better to do than spread rumors." My face felt warm. "Before I moved on the boat I asked him straight out, 'You dealing dope, Turner? 'Cause, man, I don't want any part of that. He told me he wasn't. You know why I believe him? 'Cause a guy selling dope doesn't have a beatup sailboat, that's why. He can be a jerk sometimes, but he's no smuggler, believe me." The sincerity in his eyes made me feel ashamed.

He didn't try to help when I struggled into the dinghy. "Are you going someplace to wait out the hurricane?" I asked.

"Man, don't worry about that thing." He yanked on the starter cord.

"Where are you sailing to from here?" I asked. I guess he couldn't hear me over the engine.

Nine

I HOPED ELIZABETH WOULDN'T BE MAD at me for missing dinner on *Magic*. It seemed better not to go at all than to arrive late and get the third degree. I saw our dinghy tied up to Roger's boat when Christopher dropped me off on *Emerald Eyes*. Cross-legged on deck, I trained the binoculars on *Golden Slippers*. Why did Roger and Mom go to his boat after dinner? Afraid I might show up? I could just make out two silhouettes in the cabin. What were they doing?

Soft music drifted from the boat.

"I hate you," I whispered.

I tipped my head back. It looked like a billion stars were in the sky, the Milky Way a ribbon of smoke, curling off to heaven.

I pulled myself up by a halyard and paced the deck, thinking of everything Elizabeth had said. Was the boat really too big for me? I saw myself in a stormy sea, alone. I imagined Christopher sailing *Emerald Eyes* with me. A breeze brushed the back of my neck like an icy breath. The wind seemed to sigh my name as though a voice were warning me. I shivered. *What's wrong with me?* I thought. *I can't let myself get spooked. I have this one last chance to make things up to my father. I have to save* Emerald Eyes.

I figured the hurricane would probably veer away soon, but I wasn't sure what my mother's next move would be. The hurricane threat was perfectly timed, though. Since we hadn't gone to St. Thomas to put the boat up for sale, I sensed her resolve was weakening about Venezuela. I was sure we'd sail there with *Magic* once the threat was over.

Maybe Elizabeth could keep my mother occupied while I stole away. But where could I hide in Venezuela, before sailing to the Panama Canal? I thought of my favorite anchorage near the scarlet ibis rookery. My chest hurt when I remembered the early morning vigils with my parents, watching the mangrove trees explode in a flame of scarlet as hundreds of birds burst free from their nightly roost. I remembered my mother scrambling through the mangroves, helping me search for feathers. And Daddy's laughter when he held up the egg.

Through a haze of tears I saw my mother climbing into the dinghy, Roger's voice carrying from *Golden Slippers*. I bet she didn't even remember the scarlet ibis. I rushed below and waited in my darkened cabin. Rarely did she open my door without asking. But this time I heard a click and then her soft breathing over me. I kept my eyes shut until she was gone. Only then did I turn on the light and slip the charts from my locker. I tried to muffle the *beep, beep, beep* of the GPS as I plotted alternate courses that would take me far away from her.

That night I woke with a start from a deep sleep. The full moon was framed in my overhead hatch, shining in my face. Did the light awaken me, or did I hear something? I stood on my bunk and stuck my head through the hatch, breathing the night air. The breeze felt cool against the sweat that covered my body.

At first I thought the deep drone was a mosquito, and I swatted my ear. Finally I realized it was a plane. It sounded close, and very low, but I couldn't spot it. Why would a plane be flying without lights? The sound faded and I heard waves breaking on the beach. Rain drops sprinkled my face, as I closed the hatch. I curled up in my bunk, trying to sleep, but felt oddly disturbed about the plane.

The next morning my mother was up before me, bailing overnight rain from the dinghy so the weight of the water wouldn't slow us down. Her face looked haggard as though she hadn't slept, her movements slow with fatigue. Climbing aboard, she said, "The storm's getting bigger, Molly. The winds are over a hundred and fifteen. It's a category-three hurricane."

"Is it coming toward us?" For the first time, I cared about the storm's track. I didn't want to leave Elizabeth sooner than I had to, but if I got the perfect opportunity to sneak away from Manchioneel, I might have no choice. Still I had to make sure my plotting didn't lead me smack into a major hurricane.

"It's hardly moving," Mom answered. "It's just sitting out there, growing stronger and stronger. We should have a better idea of its track later today. They expect it to start moving."

I saw Elizabeth on deck, but she didn't wave. She was definitely mad that I had gone off with Christopher.

"What time did you leave *Magic* last night?" Mom asked. "I was surprised you were already home."

I shrugged and started taking off the sail cover.

"I don't want you hanging out with that boy, Molly."

"What's wrong with him?"

"He's too old for you, for one thing. I don't like that man he crews for, either."

"I can't have a friend because you don't like the person he works for?"

"We have enough to deal with without another complication."

"Like Roger isn't a complication," I muttered.

"What does Roger have to do with this? He's our friend. He's doing everything he can to help us."

"I'll just bet," I said under my breath, yanking at the sailcover. Rainwater slid from a fold and ran down my legs.

Our three boats got underway at the same time, and we passed *Dreamer* as they were weighing anchor. When Karl had told them of our plans, they'd decided to sail to Manchioneel with us. From the bow, Peter signaled Theresa to back up because she had overrun the anchor. She slipped the throttle into reverse, and the dinghy's tow line began slipping under the stern. I shouted a warning and waved both my arms in the air, but all she did was smile and wave back.

The loud THUNK made Peter race to the helm, but the line was already fouled in the propeller and *Dreamer's* engine cut out.

Peter threw his hands in the air and looked up. "When does the fun begin?" he cried. "Who wants to buy a boat?" We circled while he pulled on his fins and mask and jumped over the side to cut the line loose. When he surfaced, blood was running down the side of his hand.

Jason yelled, "Sharks can smell blood a thousand miles away!"

Theresa clutched her chest. "Peter get out!" she screamed.

Elizabeth called out, "Dad, okay if I put a little nick in the boy and toss him over?"

My mother grabbed her mask and knife and dove in, her graceful body slicing through the water. She surfaced next to Peter and flipped her hair back.

"I'll cut the line loose," she said, adjusting her mask. "Go on up and take care of that hand." Peter looked pale as he climbed aboard. My mother dove three times, her sailing knife glinting underwater, before she finally freed the prop. Gripping the wheel, I couldn't take my eyes off her—couldn't resist the pride I felt—as she pulled herself on deck and toweled off. When her eyes caught mine, I blinked rapidly and looked away.

Peter and Theresa had to change the dinghy line and insisted we go on without them. Because their boat was much faster than any of ours, they'd catch up to us quickly. Sailing away, I saw Christopher in his dinghy, motoring up to *Dreamer.* I waved, but he didn't see me.

Standing at the bow with my binoculars, I searched for *Sinbad* and finally spotted it rocking in the remote cove. I wondered why they didn't like to anchor around other boats.

Roger began hoisting his spinnaker, the huge balloon headsail he'd sometimes fly in light wind. As the sky-blue nylon filled with air, the spinnaker revealed its surprise. In the center of the sail, Roger had painted an enormous snowy egret, its long trailing feathers flowing like a bridal veil. It had a black bill and long black legs, but its feet were bright yellow. Roger had named his boat after the snowy egret, often called "the heron with the golden slippers." He knew how much I loved his sail. I lowered my head and pretended not to see him wave.

Hundreds of bubbles filled the air and drifted over *Emerald Eyes*. They danced along the boom and skipped over the bow. Some floated just above the tops of rolling swells. I blew on them as they passed my face, making them zig into the air. Elizabeth and Jason were dipping long wands into jars of soapy water, waving them back and forth. The sun painted colorful swatches in each bubble and the breeze blew the rainbow of color over our small flotilla.

Mom gripped the wheel with both hands, shaking her head. Bubbles drifted by her face as tears ran down her cheeks. "Oh, Danny—" I heard her say, tears running down her cheek. I knew she was remembering past sails with my father when we'd blown our own bubble rainbows. I lifted my hand to a bubble. It burst when it touched my skin.

A boat came into sight in the distance, then grew quickly because of its speed. Two men were in it, a white man with long blond hair, and a West Indian with shoulder-length dreadlocks. As the boat zoomed by us, I saw four huge outboard engines along the stern. "Drug boats," Daddy used to call them. *"The only people who need boats that fast are the bad guys running away, and the good guys trying to catch them."* I watched the sleek boat, black and powerful, roaring toward Aves Island. A dark cloud crossed in front of the sun. I thought of Christopher and shivered. Seconds later, fat drops peppered the deck, and when I looked back, Aves had disappeared in a shroud of rain.

Again there were no dolphins.

From a distance, a hillside of red flowers made Manchioneel Island look as if it were on fire. As we sailed past the manchioneel trees at the entrance to Hurricane Lagoon, a shiver of foreboding raced through my body.

"Molly, is something wrong?" my mother asked. I hadn't known she was watching me.

"No," I answered, avoiding her eyes and looking away from the trees. "What could possibly be wrong?"

Young boatboys trying to earn money approached us from all directions in their old rowboats. Some of the boys were kneeling on broken surfboards, paddling hard to get to us first. Shouting urgently, they grabbed hold of *Emerald Eyes.*

"What you need, captain?" they called out in an island dialect. "You need anyting?" "Ice?" "I take your garbage."

Mom steered into the wind, the sail slapping back and forth. She pointed to the first boy who reached the boat. "We'll use you if we need anything."

"Luther, Luther," the boy said so we wouldn't forget his name and use someone else. His brown skin was the color of tamarinds. He shouted at the others to go away, swinging his thin arms at them. The others paddled hard, their ragged oars biting into the blue water, trying to reach *Magic* and *Golden Slippers* first. I dropped the main, and it folded over the boom in long even furls. We anchored in the middle of the lagoon, although my mother intended to reanchor in a much safer spot as soon as she cleared Customs and Immigration.

"I got good oysters," Luther said, holding up a tray of the small oysters he'd gathered from the roots of nearby mangroves. My mother never let me eat them—she figured I'd drop dead immediately from some fatal disease. But she used to laugh when Daddy slurped them up, because he didn't like oysters, he just wanted to give the boys some money. We bought a bunch of little bananas, and Mom paid Luther to take our trash, even though we were going ashore. He paddled away rapidly in his leaky boat, trying to reach another sailboat ahead of his friends.

There was still no sign of Peter and Theresa on *Dreamer*, and they didn't answer their radio when I called repeatedly. I hung up the microphone, trying to ignore the nervous flutter in my stomach, wondering why I was worried about them.

"You're crazy!" Elizabeth said. "You'll be killed."

"Lower your voice! You want Jason to hear us? I won't be killed unless I fall, and I'm not going to fall. Help me tie this."

The sky was black but sprinkled with stars. My mother and Roger were at a restaurant with Elizabeth's parents, and Jason was watching a video on *Magic*. I figured there would never be a better time to go up the mast.

The blue canvas mast steps went all the way to the top.

"Oh, this is great," Elizabeth snapped. "These skinny cushions around the mast will definitely help. You'll only *break* your bones instead of *pulverizing* them."

"Will you stop? I'm sorry I asked you over."

"I'm surprised you didn't ask your new friend, Christopher."

"I said I was sorry about that. It got a little late, and I figured you'd already started dinner."

"I don't like him," she grumbled.

"Now you sound like my mother. He's very nice."

She snorted and finished tying the line around my waist and the mast. I took a deep breath and stuck my foot in the first step.

"If you think you're going to barf up there, let me know so I can move."

I gritted my teeth. "Don't tempt me!"

I took another step up.

"Don't look down," she said smugly. "You might pass out."

Before I was halfway up, I did have to close my eyes. My ears hurt from the blood pounding in my head. But there was no turning back. A wake from a passing boat slapped against the hull. I hugged the mast as it swung. Halyards clanged against the aluminum mast and the sound rang in my ears. My legs trembled so hard that my foot slipped from a mast step. I probed the air until I found the webbed foothold. *I can do this*, I thought. But I couldn't. My body began to shake.

I couldn't move. Not up. Not down.

My face hurt from hugging the mast. *I have to do this*, I thought. *If I can't go up the mast to do repairs, I won't be able to sail across an ocean alone.* I don't know if I said the words— "Please help me, Daddy"—out loud, but he must have heard me, because the fear flew from my chest like a bird released from a cage. My breathing grew steady. I opened my eyes. Looking out over the dark sea, I was no longer afraid.

Then a hand grabbed my ankle.

I screamed and almost fell off the mast.

"What are you doing up here?" I yelled at Elizabeth. "Let go of my leg!"

"You've been up here forever! I kept calling you. I thought you were scared."

"I'm sorry," I said, breathless. "I'm okay now. Let's go down."

She didn't answer.

"Elizabeth?"

Her voice trembled. "I don't think I can move."

"Oh, great. You got up here, you can get down. We'll each take a step. Ready?"

"I can't, I can't."

I tried to stay calm. "Elizabeth, do you want Jason to catch us? Then the *three* of us will be up here together."

That thought was enough to get her moving. Gingerly, we climbed down, then lowered the mast steps quickly to replace the sail before my mother returned.

"Thanks for coming up like that. I just wanted to make sure I didn't have a fear of heights or anything."

She lifted her chin. "Actually I came up for the ankle bracelet. I didn't want to touch your mangled body after you fell." Climbing into the dinghy, she added, "Let's hope you never have to go up alone in the middle of a raging storm." She smiled sweetly. "When the boat's swinging like a pendulum!"

As she motored away, I looked up at the fifty-foot mast. In the dark, it seemed even higher.

Ten

Eᴀʀʟʏ ᴛʜᴇ ɴᴇxᴛ ᴍᴏʀɴɪɴɢ, we waited by the radio while Mom tried to tune the static out for a weather update. I probably looked as worried as she did, but the storm wasn't my main concern. A steady stream of boats was filling up the lagoon. With so many people around, how could I sneak away without being noticed?

"Mom, after the storm, what are we doing exactly? We're going to Venezuela with *Magic* for the rest of hurricane season, right?" She didn't answer. "Well, aren't we?"

"No," she finally said. "I've thought about it a lot and I don't want to go."

"You promised," I said, although I knew she hadn't. She didn't bother answering.

"What are we going to do?" My voice quivered.

She faced me squarely. "I still want to sail to the Virgin Islands and leave the boat with a broker, Molly." She ran her fingers through her hair. "We'll fly to the States from St. Thomas. Start our life over."

"But that means we might be giving up the boat in a few days! I thought you'd changed your mind about leaving so soon." It was hard to breathe.

"We can come back and visit sometime. Roger's invited us to vacation on *Golden Slippers* whenever we want."

I didn't trust myself to speak. No matter how many boats were around, I'd *have* to get away.

The computerized voice began the storm update, and my mother and I turned from each other. Hurricane Hank had finally stopped wobbling and was moving on a steady course. My mother began scribbling down the projected latitudes and longitudes. She paled and stopped writing. I looked at the paper. If Hurricane Hank didn't change direction, it would slam right into us.

"This is the biggest hurricane in years," she murmured. "I have a bad feeling . . ."

I felt as if my life was whirling around like a hurricane. How could I leave with a storm heading this way? But what else could I do? I didn't know my mother was watching me until she reached out and brushed a strand of hair from my face. For just a moment, forgetting everything, I let myself feel her fingers trace my skin. Then I pulled away. If I was going to save *Emerald Eyes*, I had to be careful. I grabbed the microphone and called *Dreamer* on the VHF. *Why am I so worried about them?* I wondered. Christopher was there if they needed help. I had enough to worry about with my own problems. Still it made me anxious when they didn't answer.

I heard Luther call out selling bread, and I rushed on deck. My mother bought a loaf and some homemade chutney. I bit into the warm bread and watched a chestnut race horse getting exercise in the water, a rider clinging to its back. A white star marked the center of the horse's forehead.

I saw Elizabeth climbing through her forward hatch, and I dived over the side. Underwater the horse looked as if it was running in air. I wished running away was as easy for me.

Grabbing onto *Magic*'s rail, I said, "We have to talk. That stupid hurricane might be coming this way. I don't know what I should do."

"Molly, this whole idea is crazy. I could hardly sleep last night thinking about it."

Luther pulled up in his leaky boat. "You're lucky. I have one bread left," he said, holding up a loaf. His head was level with Elizabeth's feet, and he leaned in for a closer look.

"You got a bad foot!"

Elizabeth looked down at the red toe of her white sock and let out a wail. Since Christopher's bat story she'd been wearing white socks to bed so she'd see the blood if a bat bit her.

"I vant to suck your blood!" Jason waved a bottle of red nail polish, then whirled from Elizabeth's grip. He leaped into the water still in his cotton shorty pajamas and hung onto the side of Luther's boat.

"Elizabeth has bat rabies!" Jason sang, both boys laughing hard. I remembered how once I'd wished for a little sister or brother. Now the thought gave me the creeps.

Elizabeth and I went ashore as soon as we could. The town was getting ready for one of its festivals. Men and teenagers dragged long tables from the backs of pickup trucks, while others wheeled supplies from nearby homes. Women set up metal cooking vats, and children helped stack wooden folding chairs against the trees. They told us there would be food and music the next night, but they'd also be giving information about storm shelters and other safety suggestions.

We hurried toward a fancy tourist hotel to escape Jason. He trailed behind, playing with some local children and showing off his dead shark. We ran up the redwood steps to the hotel swimming pool. A small sign said, "For Hotel Guests Only," but no one was around to chase us away. We sat under umbrellas in lounge chairs. Yellow bananaquits, called sugar birds, were poking into small dishes of sugar left out for them on poolside tables.

"I've been thinking," Elizabeth said quickly. "It's really hard living on a boat sometimes. I haven't gotten mail for two whole months. It's sitting in Venezuela!"

I opened my mouth.

"Wait, let me finish." She looked at me from the corner of her eye. "I mean, I love living on *Magic*, but sometimes . . . I don't know, I guess I just wish we had a little house." She shifted her eyes, as though waiting for my reaction. I had no idea what her point was. "No, a *big* house—with my bedroom on the opposite wing from Jason's. And a telephone. And friends who live down the street. At least houses can't sail away."

She chewed her lip, then blurted out, "It would be *great* if you moved into a house, Molly. I could visit you."

I rolled my eyes. "Oh, now I get it. Well, I'm taking *Emerald Eyes*, so just forget it." I got up and jumped into the pool.

She slid into the water and faced me. "Molly, please don't steal your boat."

"It's *my* boat, Elizabeth. I'm not a boat thief."

"You know what I mean."

"I think I've figured out what to do. Do you want to hear or don't you?"

She nodded grudgingly.

I looked around to make sure Jason wasn't sneaking up on us.

"My mother said as soon as this hurricane thing is over, we're sailing to the Virgin Islands and leaving the boat with a broker."

Elizabeth looked heartbroken. "You're not coming to Venezuela with us for the rest of the hurricane season? You said she changed her mind."

"I thought she did. But all she wants to do is get rid of *Emerald Eyes*. She doesn't care about the boat. Or my father."

"Oh, Molly . . ."

"We'll have to fly to Puerto Rico from St. Thomas for a connecting flight to New York. That's where I'll do it."

"Do what?"

"Slip away from my mother and go *back* to St. Thomas. It's only about a half-hour by plane. She'll never suspect where I've gone. By the time she figures it out, I'll be far away. What do you think?"

"Hmm. It would be a great idea . . . if it wasn't so dumb."

"What's dumb about it?"

"Well, for one thing, you need a plane ticket. Where will you get the money?"

I hesitated, still ashamed to admit my theft. "I have birthday money left," I answered.

"How much money did you *get* for your birthday? Your grandmother must be rich."

"Will you forget the money, Elizabeth? What about my plan?"

"Your *dumb* plan you mean! Your mother will have a

thousand people searching for you, two seconds after you're gone."

"I could leave her a note. Say I'm going to visit all Daddy's favorite places before we leave Puerto Rico."

She nodded. "I guess you could say that. Or you could tell her you just have to be alone for a while."

"Right. I'll say I'm staying in a hotel for two weeks to be by myself."

"And while your mother's searching in Puerto Rico, you'll have time to—" Elizabeth slapped her head. "I can't believe I just did that. Helped you come up with a plan for this stupid idea."

"It's not stupid."

"It is, Molly. You can't just drift around out there. Where are you going?"

"Tahiti."

"Tahiti?" She smacked the water with both hands. "I knew it. An alien being has invaded my friend's body. Get the Raid." She glared at me. "You intend to sail across the entire Pacific Ocean all by yourself?"

I swam away from her and she dog-paddled after me.

"That's brilliant, Molly. Don't worry about a whale attack while you're out there." She kept swimming behind me. "But just in case a whale sinks *Emerald Eyes*, and you're adrift in a lifeboat, bring a spoon so you can scoop out fish eyes and suck the liquid from them when you're dying of thirst and frying in the sun." She made a slurping noise. "Fish eyes, yum yum."

"Are you finished?" I snapped.

"I will never speak to you again if you do this."

"I can do it, Elizabeth. I can."

"And what if you have to put in somewhere in Colombia before you get to the Panama Canal? We know of two cruisers who were killed by drug dealers when they had to anchor in a remote place in the middle of the night. They didn't have guns to protect themselves, and neither do you."

A little bell went off in my mind.

She narrowed her eyes. "What are you thinking?"

I shook my head. "Nothing," I answered quickly. "I'm sailing to Panama, going through the canal, then I'll just . . . I'll just do it. I'll sail the boat to the South Pacific like Tania."

"You can't sail across the Pacific Ocean by yourself, Molly. Suppose you get sick? Suppose you get *hurt*? You could get gangrene. You might have to saw your own leg off!"

"Will you stop? You're scaring me."

"I'm not going to let you sail away by yourself!"

"Fine! Why don't you come with me?"

Her eyes widened and she shook her head vigorously. "I can't go, Molly, honest. I'd be too scared, and my parents would kill me."

"Suppose someone else goes with me?" I just wanted to hear the words out loud. Toss them around like seaglass. See if they sparkled—or cut.

"Like who?" she asked.

"Hey, you guys," Jason called. "I've been looking all over for you."

"My brother!" Elizabeth said. "Take him, Molly, please. Just promise you won't bring him back."

"Take me where?" Jason asked. He kicked off his sneakers and jumped in the pool, his legs angled like a skinny frog's.

Elizabeth almost leaped on me while Jason was underwater. "What are you thinking?" she asked. "You're not thinking of asking that guy Christopher to go with you?"

"No, of course not. Don't worry, I wouldn't go with anyone but you." *Besides,* I thought, *I'll probably never see him again.*

Bougainvillea petals floated in the pool, and we blew them back and forth to each other. Jason released his bottled shark and dove, trying to catch it as it drifted toward the blue-tiled bottom. Elizabeth watched me closely, but we couldn't talk anymore with Jason so near. We swam for a while longer, then showered under a cool fountain, and slipped on our clothes.

What if I *do* see Christopher again? He wants to sail his brother and sisters around the world. Be a family. I wonder where he is.

"Why do you have that look on your face?" Elizabeth asked. I didn't tell her. And I didn't mention another thought on my mind, something I would have to do right away. If I told Elizabeth—no, I couldn't tell her. It was too frightening, even to me. There are some things even a best friend won't keep secret.

Eleven

From THE POOL we followed the landscaped path that circled the hotel property. Hummingbirds, iridescent green and purple, flitted in and out of drooping red blossoms like fat bees. Two squawking blackbirds flew ahead from tree to tree, trying to lead us away from a hidden nest. A flock of parrots filled the air with their chatter. Purple bougainvillea draped the hillside like a long, satin sheet. The hotel's nature walk was one of the reasons I loved the island. Mom and I used to pick one blossom each on our walks and later press them into our ship's log. I stuck out my tongue and tried to taste the sweet fragrance of frangipani. I fed a red hibiscus to an iguana, dropping the blossom on the ground in front of his mouth so he wouldn't bite my fingers accidentally. He snatched it up, chewing slowly, then swished into the bushes like a bored dragon.

Jason came running back to us. "Hey, I just found a dirt path behind those gumbo-limbo trees. Let's follow it." He showed us the overgrown entrance, hidden in the heavy foliage. We ducked under some branches and crawled to a narrow dirt path where we were able to stand. The trees formed a dense ceiling that blocked the sun. Thick brown vines hung to the ground like long stringy hair. The path was dark and damp.

"This is creepy. Let's get out of here," Elizabeth said.

"Please, please," Jason begged. "Let's just see where it goes. Maybe there's a house at the end. Come on."

It didn't get any better. The deeper we walked, the darker it got. Large boulders, taller than our heads, bordered one side of the walk. They were dark brown and scored deeply, like the back of an old sailor's neck.

Fat crabs scuttled sideways across the path as we crept deeper into the bush. A loud buzzing made Elizabeth grab my arm. Even Jason stepped back, the hem of Elizabeth's shirt bunched in his fist. Hundreds of green flies crawled through a dead crab, eating its insides. The flies swarmed into the air, around my nose and mouth.

Elizabeth and I stared in horror. Jason grinned.

"Wow! Just like Hansel and Gretel," he said, moving forward. Dead crabs, lying on their backs, marked the path like bread crumbs.

"Hansel and Gretel?" Elizabeth hissed, glaring at him. "Hansel left bread crumbs so they could find their way *out* of the forest! We are following dead crabs *into* the forest! I'm getting out of here." As she started to turn, we heard voices. Jason crept ahead, and we followed him, stepping gingerly over the dead crabs that led the way.

The voices got louder, and we could see movement beyond the trees. We knelt down, crawled toward the light, then pushed the low branches aside. We had come to a small cove where boats never anchored because it was exposed to the sea and the easterly trade winds.

Sinbad was almost hidden in the tangled trees near shore. Turner was on deck, Christopher in the dinghy with a brush and bucket of paint. I figured he intended to paint the scrape along the hull. Big swells rocked the dinghy, and he hung on to *Sinbad*, trying not to spill paint. He put the can down and picked up a thick roll of green edging tape.

"What are they doing anchored here?" Jason whispered.

"They like privacy," I answered.

A cigarette dangled from Turner's mouth, his black hair loose around his shoulders like the vines choking our trail. Jason leaned into me for a better look and knocked me over. My hand pressed on a burr and I yelped.

Turner flicked his cigarette into the water and called to Christopher. "Hey, somebody's in there!"

I don't know why I got frightened, why I wanted to follow Elizabeth when she started backing up. I only know that the fear made me feel guilty. I stood and stepped out into the open.

Surprise flickered in Christopher's eyes when he saw me, then anger. "What are you doing here?" I don't know if he deliberately dropped the tape or if it slipped from his hands. Waves lifted and tossed the dinghy, and Christopher almost fell over.

"We were just exploring," I answered, hurt by his tone. "And we heard voices." Jason and Elizabeth stood up on either side of me. We were so close, a feather couldn't slip between us.

Elizabeth crossed her arms. "What are *you* doing here?" she demanded.

Turner lit another cigarette and flipped his match toward us. "You writing a book, too?" he asked.

Christopher's face cleared, and he smiled suddenly.

"We're just getting the boat ready," he said. "If the hurricane doesn't change course, we'll take it out to sea."

"Out to sea?" I cried. "Isn't that dangerous?"

"It's a lot more dangerous to anchor near other boats," he said. "They'll drag right into you. That's how you end up sinking. You have a much better chance if you take your boat out to sea." *Out to sea*, I thought. *I never knew a boat was safer at sea in a hurricane.*

"I bet you puke your brains out," Jason said, grinning.

Christopher didn't take the bait. He began stirring the paint with a flat stick. Was he deliberately ignoring us?

"We have to go," I said sullenly.

He flashed a warm smile. "I doubt we'll really get a hurricane. But good luck just in case."

"You, too," I answered.

"Good luck puking your brains out," Jason said. "Don't worry Turner, you have no brains so you won't pu—" Elizabeth clamped her hand over his mouth. A fleeting smile crossed Christopher's face, but I thought he tried to hide it.

"Take a hike," Turner snapped.

We backed up, then turned and raced along the path, vines snagging in my hair like clutching fingers. My heart was pounding, but not from the dead crabs that crunched underfoot, not even from trying to keep up with Elizabeth and Jason. A new thought left me breathless: *A boat is safer in a hurricane if you take it out to sea.*

When we returned, a white Coast Guard cutter, with a broad orange band on the bow, was anchored in Hurricane Lagoon, and a boarding party of three men and a woman in a black inflatable launch, pulled alongside *Emerald Eyes*.

Many live-aboard cruisers get angry when the Coast Guard boards to check safety equipment. The police need a search warrant to go into houses, but our cruising homes could be invaded anytime without cause. Daddy didn't mind, though, I guess because he had been a policeman for so long.

One of the Coast Guard glanced into my dinghy as I pulled up. I was glad Mom always kept the lifejackets hooked at the bow. The boarding party climbed onto *Emerald Eyes* after me. Mom already had the pouch out with our ship's papers. It was unusual to get boarded in a foreign port. It had only happened to us once before, in Grenada, when the Coast Guard had spent a week in St. George's harbor and boarded all the American vessels.

"How come you're here?" I asked them as they filled out forms in the cockpit.

"We're doing some training," he answered.

"I heard some fishermen talking on shore earlier," my mother said. "Someone found a large bale of marijuana floating near Aves Island. Anything we need to worry about?" A small shock went through me, as if I'd touched a frayed wire. I remembered the plane I'd heard late at night. Had it been dropping marijuana? I remembered the black speed boat I'd seen racing to Aves the next day.

"We'll be around this area for a while," the man said, evasively. He looked at Mom, then me. "You haven't noticed anything unusual have you?"

I swallowed and shook my head hard. Were Christopher and Turner hiding in that cove? I wondered. And where was *Dreamer*? The last time I saw it, Christopher was climbing aboard. I remembered the hungry look in his face when he gazed at *Dreamer*. Had he done something to Peter and Theresa? Stolen their boat? My stomach felt as if it were filled with sand. Something else was bothering me, too—something Christopher had said when we found him in the cove. But I couldn't think of what it was.

Everything on the boat satisfied Coast Guard requirements: Our flares, radio license, and ship's papers were up to date, and we had the necessary signs attached to the bulkheads about the prohibition on discharging oil and dumping plastic trash. They marked "no violations" on the form and handed us a copy before leaving.

"There's *Dreamer!*" I shouted.

"They sailed in a little while ago," my mother said. "Why do you sound so surprised?"

I didn't answer as guilt washed over me. I would never be suspicious of Christopher again.

Late that night I entered my parents' cabin for the first time since Daddy died. The breeze through the overhead hatch felt like a breath across my shoulder. My mother was at Roger's, listening to the latest weather update. At least that's what she wanted me to believe. My hands reached for the locker door as though a ghost had control of my body. The air-tight box was cold against my fingers. My mouth was so dry I could barely swallow. I lifted the lid. It was still there inside the box. That was all I needed to know. I never meant to take it out. A drop of sweat splashed on my thumb. With trembling fingers I unfolded the cloth. I never heard the steps behind me. It was a creaking floorboard that made me spin around.

"Oh, my God—" My mother leaped out of the way.

The gun in my hand was pointed at her heart.

Her hand shook even more than mine as she pushed

the barrel aside and pulled the gun out of my hand.

I'd never seen her so angry, so frightened. Not even when my father was drinking. For a moment I thought she would hit me. Instead she began to cry.

"What were you thinking? What possible reason—"

I was so scared myself, I could barely think. "I . . . I was just wondering if Daddy had taken it with him. That's all."

"You *know* not to touch your father's gun. We had it for emergencies only! It's not a toy! You've never done something like this. What's wrong with you?" She turned and marched away with the gun.

"Where are you going?"

"I'm taking it out in the dinghy. I'm throwing it over—"

"Don't! I'll never touch it again, I swear." Lying was getting easier and easier.

I raced up the stairs after her. I wanted to plead with her to keep the gun, not only because I might need it in dangerous anchorages, but because the gun—the police force—had been so much a part of my father's life. But I was afraid of arousing her suspicion. I watched her motor out to deep water. I imagined my father's gun spinning, spinning, to a dark grave far below, as my mother drifted further and further away. Watching her shoulders shake in the moonlight, I thought I would tremble into pieces and blow away.

Twelve

THE NEXT DAY MY MOTHER SAID Roger was picking her up that night for the festival, so I could have the dinghy. She didn't say a word about the gun.

"Are you getting all dressed up?" I asked.

She turned to me. "I don't know what I'm wearing. Why?"

I didn't answer. Instead I asked, "Why don't we go out to sea for the hurricane?"

She choked on a mouthful of tea. "Out to *sea*? Why would you even ask something like that?"

"Isn't it safer? Suppose another boat hits us here? It could destroy *Emerald Eyes*. Nothing can hit us in the middle of the ocean, right?"

She was shaking her head the whole time I spoke. "This storm is monstrous. The winds are up to 160 miles an hour, and gusts are over 200. It's a category five! I wouldn't want to be caught in a storm *half* that size."

"If we left right away, it could miss us."

"There's absolutely no way of knowing what a storm like this is going to do. Only an idiot would sail into the teeth of this thing."

"Suppose another boat sinks us in the anchorage?"

"We're insured," she answered.

The sunglasses hid my angry eyes.

Not many people had arrived when Elizabeth and I got to shore, but grills were lit and pots were already steaming along the street. The air was filled with delicious West Indian cooking smells: barbecue chicken and ribs, salt fish, conch rotis, and meat pates. A West Indian man stirred a big pot of thick callalu soup, my favorite, but the thought of the land crabs that flavor the soup made my stomach flip.

Elizabeth and I hurried by. We ate chicken and sweet potato stuffing, bought some johnnycakes and sodas, and walked to a bench near a gnarled banyon tree away from the square and other people.

"Molly, can I ask you something?" Elizabeth was nibbling an end of the hot fry bread. "It's about your father," she said.

A skinny dog sniffed at our shoes. I scuffed the ground with my foot, and the dog jumped back, frightened. I tossed him a piece of johnnycake, and he wolfed it down and slunk off with his tail between his legs.

"I was just wondering how your Dad died. I know a little bit . . . If it's too upsetting," she added quickly, "you don't have to tell me."

I was sure I couldn't tell her. But my feelings surprised me. For the first time, I knew I could talk about my father.

More than that, I *wanted* to talk about him. "He was help-ing some men bring a sailboat to the States," I said slow-ly. "The boat was in terrible condition. They ran into a really bad storm. One of the lifelines gave way. He must have been leaning on it." *Was he drinking?* I wondered. "One minute my father was on deck . . . and then he was gone." *Gone.* A tear ran into my mouth. "By the time they got him back on the boat, it was too late."

"Oh, Molly." Elizabeth scooted close to me.

"He wasn't wearing his life jacket and harness," I said. "It was all my fault, Elizabeth."

"You weren't even there, Molly," she said softy. "How could it be your fault?"

I closed my eyes and remembered. *We have just returned to the boat after crossing the shark pool. Daddy stum-bles into the cabin and smiles at my mother. "Molly's sailing with me tomorrow." His voice is thick, his words slurred.*

Mom comes closer. She doesn't answer. She's staring at Daddy, and her lips have gone white. I think she looks like a wild animal, and if Daddy makes a wrong move, she'll back down on her haunches and spring through the air.

"Over my dead body," she says. Her words crackle the air. Even Daddy doesn't open his mouth.

"Over my dead body," she repeats, even more quietly, and steps between us.

My breath came in gulps and Elizabeth hugged me tightly. I wanted to tell her the whole truth, but I was too ashamed. How could I tell anyone how *relieved* I was that my mother wouldn't let me go? How could I tell anyone about the following morning?

Before my father left, I'd heard their raised voices in the cabin. I couldn't make out the words, but I knew they were fighting about me. What if my mother gave in and let me go? Daddy opened my cabin door. I heard his breathing. I pretended to be asleep. Even when he brushed my hair back and kissed my forehead, I kept perfectly still. He whispered, "I love you, McGoo. Take care of *Emerald Eyes*." I held my breath until he was gone. I never said goodbye. And I never saw him again.

I lifted my head from Elizabeth's shoulder. "If I'd been with him, I wouldn't have let him go on deck without a life jacket. We always reminded each other about that."

"You could have been washed overboard, too, Molly. Your father would never have wanted you on that junky boat."

"He wanted me to go with him," I said. She looked surprised.

I'll make it up to him, I thought. I felt a warning stir in my mind, a warning as clear as my father whispering, "I love you, McGoo." But I wasn't ready to listen. *Don't worry, Daddy*, I thought. *I won't let you down again.*

The festival was in full swing. Bending at the waist, Elizabeth and I munched on hot corn-on-the-cob, trying to keep the butter from running down our chins and onto our shirts. Teenagers and younger kids in the steel band pounded out rocking calypso on their pans. Luther and two other boat boys played with them. Crowds of people—West Indians, visiting sailors, tourists who hadn't been able to get flights out before the storm—thronged the street and square. Thwack! Thwack! A group of laughing men slapped dominoes on a table.

Elizabeth shook my arm violently and sent the corn cob flying. A stray dog caught it in midair and crept away.

"Look!" she said, pointing. Christopher was deep in conversation with a man who looked vaguely familiar.

"I think Christopher's nuts for going out to sea. Don't you?" Elizabeth asked.

"Mmmm," I murmured, watching him. His words kept gnawing at my mind: "A boat is safer at sea in a hurricane." We were too far away to hear, but the other man looked angry. Christopher seemed upset, too—or was he excited? Why did the other man look so familiar? It was something about his hair. An electrical short made the loud speaker blast the air, and the noise triggered my memory: the speedboat with the four giant engines! One of the men in it had long blond hair—just like the man with Christopher.

"Come on," I said. "Let's go talk to him."

"Molly!" Mom called from down the street.

"Parents have radar," Elizabeth whispered.

My mother was standing under a line of colored lanterns. She looked so pretty, like she was at the end of a rainbow, the colors spilling in her hair and across her face.

"Come and say hello to Risa." I turned back toward the beach, but Christopher had already gone.

Risa was a beautiful black woman, almost six-feet tall, who owned a small hotel and a few guest cottages. Before she married a West Indian man and moved to Manchioneel, she'd been a model in New York. The first time we sailed to the island, she heard us in the square. "It sure is nice to hear a New York accent," she said. "I get homesick here in paradise—for about two minutes a year." My father's laugh made her smile. Risa's husband died before we ever met him, but she never left Manchioneel.

She walked toward me, her face solemn. Her head was

completely shaved, and she wore large, gold hoop earrings. Her red and gold batik sarong was draped over one shoulder, leaving the other bare, and the material flowed all the way to the ground. She looked like an African queen.

Risa held my face between her hands. "Oh, sweet thing," she whispered. "What was the good Lord thinking, taking your daddy away?" She kissed my forehead and slid her thumbs across the tears under my eyes. "Don't you worry, honey. Your daddy's in heaven right now, watching over you."

"This is my friend, Elizabeth," I said, backing away before I started bawling.

Risa sniffed, then nodded abruptly like she knew why I had to change the subject. She shook Elizabeth's hand. "I like your style, honey. Those are the fanciest toenails I've ever seen."

"Thanks. Take off your sneakers, Molly. Show her yours."

"That's okay," Risa said. "I'll take your word for it." She turned to me and smiled. "The ponies will be real happy to see you, Molly."

The first time we went to her house, two Great Danes were sleeping in her bed, and I thought they were ponies. She had cats everywhere, too. Daddy slipped his hand under a sleeping cat and held it up. It draped over his hand like a stuffed animal, the head and back feet hanging down together. "Honey Man, wake up!" Risa had said in the cat's ear, but it didn't even stir. She and Daddy howled with laughter.

"Can I bring Elizabeth over to see the dogs?" I asked her.

"Well, of course she's coming over. You're all coming."

I saw Roger approaching. "Thanks, Risa," I said, hurrying away with Elizabeth before my mother could stop me. I spotted Christopher across the street. He was leaning against a tree and watching me, a bottle of beer in his hand. Before I could reach him, he melted into the crowd.

People were dancing in the square and mako jumbies on stilts were weaving through the crowd. Luther came running up with another man. "You dead of foot rabies yet?" he asked Elizabeth, grinning.

She let soda dribble from her mouth. Her mother waved her over to another stand. "Be right back, Molly."

"This is my cousin," Luther said. "He drives a taxi, the best one on the island. You should take a tour right away. I get you all a good price."

"You were riding the horse with the star on its head!" I exclaimed.

"When this nasty Hank business is gone away, I give you a good tour of the island," the man said.

"Not for free, though," Luther cautioned.

The man smiled. "Luther has made himself my new agent."

"You think the hurricane will really hit us?" I asked.

The man looked over my shoulder, and the smile left his face. "There are some who do more evil than a hurricane," he said. Turning, I saw the blond-haired man just before he disappeared in the crowd. Luther dragged his cousin to a food stall before I could ask if he was talking about Christopher's friend.

Nearby, my mother stood with Roger. Her green and black sarong, tied at the waist, hung softly to her knees. A white silk tank top showed the outline of her small breasts. When she and Roger laughed together, an ache filled my chest. Out of nowhere someone's hands clamped on my shoulders, and I spun around. It was Christopher.

"You scared me," I said.

"I seem to do that a lot."

"Are you still sailing out to sea with Turner?"

He looked puzzled.

"You were getting the boat ready, remember?

He tipped a beer bottle to his mouth, then rubbed his lips with the back of his hand. "Turner had an emergency. Someone in his family got sick and he had to leave the island."

"That's terrible." Turner gave me the creeps, but I didn't want anything bad to happen to him or his family. "Is that what that guy was telling you? The one with the blond hair?"

His eyes shone as he nodded. "Yeah. Now I have Turner's boat to worry about."

The inside of my head was humming. "What are you going to do? Will you go out to sea by yourself? It's a good idea to do that, right?" *Should I follow when he leaves?*

"I don't know what I'm doing." He frowned and ran his hand through his hair. "I still think this storm is going to miss us. Turner was sure of it."

"Oh, well, if you're not going, you'd better bring the boat into Hurricane Lagoon, just in case," I said. "It's getting filled up with boats."

He looked into the harbor. A small pulse ticked near one of his eyes. "Yeah, well, even if I wanted to, I couldn't come yet."

"Why not?"

He hesitated, then shrugged. "The entrance is too tricky to come in at night. You want a beer?"

Mom walked up and I wondered if Elizabeth was right, that she did have some kind of radar. Everyone followed Mom over, even Peter and Theresa. Karl and Gina were chatting with Risa like they'd known each other forever.

Peter said, "Another couple of fouled props, and I might *give* you the boat, Christopher, instead of selling it to you someday. And now a hurricane. Unbelievable."

"Don't you think it'll change course?" Christopher asked.

Roger said, "Even if it's not a direct hit, we'll get a nasty piece of it. The hurricane-force winds extend out pretty far. The sustained winds are over 160 miles an hour. And it's still getting worse."

Christopher looked frightened, which surprised me. "Turner said a hurricane hasn't hit here in years. He was *certain* it wouldn't affect us."

"Well, he's a fool," my mother snapped.

"Mom," I complained. "Turner had to leave because someone in his family got sick."

Not the least contrite, she stared at Christopher. "Where's the boat? I hope you had sense enough to get it in the mangroves."

"Mom, don't be so mean."

Risa placed her hand on my arm. She was studying Christopher, but then looked at me. "Your friend's welcome to stay with us, too," Risa said.

"Stay with you when?" I asked.

"Risa's invited us to stay with her during the hurricane instead of going to a shelter," my mother answered.

"A shelter?"

"Are you kidding?" Christopher said. "I'm not abandoning the boat in a hurricane."

"Then you're a fool like your friend!" my mother said.

"What are you talking about, Mom? We have to stay on *Emerald Eyes*. Who's going to take care of her during the hurricane?"

My mother's mouth fell open. "We can't stay aboard,

Molly. It never even occurred to me you thought we would. This storm is a category five, the worst there is. It's a killer."

Jason looked up at his father. "Aren't we staying on *Magic*, Dad?"

"No, son. We'll take Risa up on her kind offer. The storm's too dangerous now, like Jennie said."

"Mom, we can't leave the boat all alone," I said urgently. "She might get destroyed."

"Molly, this storm is still strengthening. The gusts are over 200 miles an hour. There's absolutely nothing anyone can do in winds like that. Nothing. You couldn't even stand on deck." She reached out to touch my arm, and I swung it behind me.

"Dad would stay on *Emerald Eyes* no matter how bad the hurricane was."

Everyone got quiet. "Maybe he would, Molly. But he wouldn't have before he started—" She stopped, knowing the others were listening. "He might have stayed on it himself, Molly. But never, *never*, would he have allowed you to stay on board in a storm." She took a step toward me and I backed away.

I heard Christopher's voice. "Well I can tell you one thing. I wouldn't abandon *Sinbad* in a hurricane, and it doesn't even belong to me."

My mother whirled on him. "What's wrong with you? Don't you have any brains in your head?"

His face was red and I realized he was a little drunk. He moved closer to me, and my mother pushed him—actually put her hand against his chest—and shoved him away from me.

"You almost killed yourself with that reef trick. And now you want to harm my child with your stupidity?"

"Mom, stop it!" I yelled. Elizabeth squeezed my hand.

Christopher held his hands out, palms up. "Obviously I'm not wanted around here," he said to my mother. But when he looked at me, there was a light in his eyes, as if he were trying to tell me something before he walked away.

"You had no right to talk to him like that!" I shouted.

"No, you're right," she said, surprising me. She pressed her palms against her eyes. "I just lost my head. I don't know what's wrong with me."

"There's nothing wrong with you, honey," Risa said. "You've got a child to worry about, that's all."

"I'm staying on *Emerald Eyes*," I said through my clenched teeth.

"We're not!" my mother shouted. "It's unsafe! We're staying at Risa's!"

Roger stepped toward me. "Molly—"

I ran to the dinghy and left everyone behind, even Elizabeth, and raced home to *Emerald Eyes*.

Thirteen

BEFORE LONG JASON and Elizabeth motored up.

"Are you okay?" Elizabeth asked.

"Come on over," Jason said. "We'll watch a scary movie on the VCR."

Elizabeth rolled her eyes. "We're *not* watching anything scary, Jason. Come on over, Molly. Don't stay here all by yourself."

"Want us to come up?" Jason asked. He had little wrinkles between his eyes, and I knew he felt bad about the fight with my mother.

"I just feel like being alone for awhile."

"I'll wait up in case you want me to come stay with you. Okay?" Elizabeth reached up and took my hand.

"I'm okay, really. I just want to be by myself."

They motored toward *Magic*, Elizabeth watching me over her shoulder the whole way.

Huddled at the bow, I rested my chin on my knees and watched little underwater creatures journey past the boat, leaving bright phosphorescent trails. I wished I could slip into the water and float away with them. The Coast Guard cutter was still anchored in Hurricane Lagoon. The moon made the water around it sparkle like ground glass. I wasn't surprised when Christopher paddled up in Luther's leaky boat. He rested his arms on the varnished rail, his head level with my lap. Should I follow him out to sea if he goes? Or ask him to sail away with me on *Emerald Eyes* afterward? I almost pressed my thumb against the nervous tic near his eye. But I clasped my hands in my lap.

"I'm sorry about what happened before," he said. "But your mother is really uptight."

His remark annoyed me. Then I remembered he didn't know about my father. "I didn't tell you the truth about something. My father isn't away. He . . . he died recently."

"Oh, man, now I really feel bad. But maybe I can make it up to you."

I waited.

"I'm in a mess with Turner gone." There was a spark of excitement in his eyes, maybe fear as well. "Now I've got to do something with the boat. I feel obligated, you know, to help him out. I'm going to bring *Sinbad* around to this harbor tomorrow. It's too late to go out to sea."

"It is? But I thought—"

"Can you give me a quick hand with the anchoring and stuff when I get here?" He licked his lips nervously. "And when we're done, we'll come right to your boat, *Emerald Eyes*, and we'll stay on it during the hurricane. I'll help you take care of it. What do you say?"

"You'd do that? Stay on my boat instead of Turner's?"

His eyes never wavered. "Absolutely. Once I anchor his boat, my obligation to him is over." I hesitated and he said, "Look, I know how you feel about your boat. I could tell. I want to help you with this. You were really nice to me. Letting me blabber about my family and all. It's the least I can do for you."

The question popped out of my mouth, as though it had a life of its own: "If you had your own boat, would you sail to someplace like . . . Tahiti? Do you think your brother and sisters would like that?"

"Tahiti? I never thought about it. Sure, why not? I helped some guy bring his boat from Colombia to the Panama Canal. He was sailing to Tahiti."

"You were in Colombia"

A flashlight blinked on and off on *Magic*, and I knew Elizabeth was signaling. I spotted my mother and Roger motoring from shore. "You'd better go," I said.

"Say you'll meet me!" He gripped my wrist and leaned close.

My heart was racing. "What if I can't get away?"

"You can do it. For your father. He'd want you to protect the boat, wouldn't he?" I smelled the beer on his breath. But he was offering to help me save *Emerald Eyes*. And he was counting on me to help him. How could I refuse?

That night I dreamed that a whispering voice lured me into the dark. I came to the shark pool at Calabash, only now it was filled with killer sharks. Black fins cut silently through the surface of the water on both sides of the path, gliding back and forth near my feet. I tried to turn back, but the whisper pulled me closer. I saw a shadow at the other end of the walk. Someone dangerous was waiting for me, but I couldn't see his face. He reached out to me, and I stepped forward, but the ground turned to water beneath my feet. The shark fins glided toward me. Over and over, I heard a new voice calling my name, someone trying to save me.

"Molly." Mom shook me gently and pulled me up from the nightmare. "Molly, honey, it's all right," she said. "You were having a bad dream." She wiped the wet hair from my face and I lay there, feigning sleep. She ran the back of her hand up and down on my cheek like she'd always done when I was a little girl. I felt her warm breath on my face as she leaned over and kissed my cheek. When she closed the cabin door, tears ran into my ears. I rolled over and buried my face in the pillow. I listened to the lively jingling of the tree frogs along the shore until I fell asleep.

The sky was overcast when I awoke, but later it cleared, and I figured the weather bureau was wrong after all. I watched my mother sip coffee, reading her meditation book. I wished I could tell her how frightened I was and put my head in her lap like I had when I was a little girl. But when she asked about my nightmare, I pretended not to remember.

I looked around the lagoon. Boaters had sailed from all over to tie into the mangrove roots that surrounded the entire lagoon. The twisting roots grew deep in the ground and wove a steel-like net around the shore. Even if anchors dragged in the storm, the roots would keep the boats from blowing away. Those boaters who arrived late had to anchor in the middle of the lagoon. If their anchors dragged, they could smash into the boats tied to the mangroves—unless someone was on board to push the boats away.

In spite of my pleas, Mom still refused to stay on board and take care of *Emerald Eyes*. In fact, she finally refused to discuss it. In silence, we spent the entire morning stripping the boat from bow to stern, storing everything below, even removing the mainsail from the boom so the wind couldn't shred it.

Local fishing boats were anchored everywhere, their island flags already lowered. I saw a Norwegian flag flying from the stern of a boat that I remembered from Bonaire. I recognized flags from Israel, Great Britain, Spain, Finland, Sweden, Denmark, and Germany—even a Rising Sun from Japan. And there were other Canadian and U.S. boats besides *Magic* and *Emerald Eyes*. A French couple, untying their blue, white, and red flag from the backstay of their steel sloop, waved as I folded up our flag. It was as if we were now part of one nation—a nation under siege.

But where was *Sinbad*? Why hadn't Christopher arrived?

We were tucked in so close to shore on both sides that branches brushed the deck. We had three anchors off the bow, and we were still crawling in the mangroves weaving extra lines through roots that were as thick as my arm. We added extra chafing gear, too, so the lines wouldn't wear through and cast us adrift. Every now and then I'd check for Christopher, but there was still no sign of him.

Finally, there were no more boats coming into the harbor, and the Coast Guard cutter left. Everyone worked feverishly completing last-minute preparations on deck. Soon we would feel the first effects of the storm.

When we finished, my mother took a last swim. As she did a slow crawl to *Golden Slippers*, I pulled the mask over my face and slipped silently into the water. I floated on the surface and watched an upside-down jellyfish come to life.

Then I swam toward *Golden Slippers*.

Underwater, I could see my mother from the shoulders down, Roger beside her. I saw him place his hand on my mother's waist. Maybe he was just moving her away from the boarding ladder that was brushing her back. But he left his hand there. I let my breath out and began to sink as the air emptied from my lungs. My body felt cold, like I was drowning in ice water.

I swam back to *Emerald Eyes* and climbed on deck. I couldn't take my eyes off my mother as she smiled at Roger. The water on her face glistened in the sun.

Toweling off, I watched them swim toward me.

Roger gripped the rail near my feet. "Hey, McGoo," he said, smiling. Even my mother winced at the sound of my father's pet name. Roger started climbing up after her.

"Don't you *dare* come on this boat!" I cried.

He fell back as if I'd pushed him.

"Don't you *ever* touch my mother again."

"Molly!" my mother yelled.

Roger was treading backwards, his eyes filled with shock and hurt.

I rushed below, my mother at my heels. "What is in your head? What are you thinking?" She grabbed my shoulders and shook me. "That Roger and I . . ."

I twisted out of her hands. "I know what's been going on between you."

"Nothing! That's what's been going on. Nothing!"

"I've been watching you. Roger this, Roger that, your head on his shoulder—'You're so *sweet*, Roger; I can't *wait* to sell the boat, Roger.'—Don't tell me, 'nothing.'"

She dropped into a seat, her eyes filled with confusion,

maybe surprise. But she didn't deny it. She just sat there staring at me, as if she hadn't even known how close she was getting to Roger until I told her.

"You should have let me go with Daddy. I could have saved him. I wasn't afraid to go with him. *I wasn't!*"

Her mouth opened, her eyes grew wide in astonishment. And I felt her look right into my soul and see my secret.

"Oh, Molly, I had no idea—" She pressed my hands between hers like in prayer. "It's okay if you were afraid to go with Daddy. Don't feel guilty. You're a young girl. You should have been afraid. Fear teaches us caution."

"I said I *wasn't* afraid. You drove him away." I pulled my hands loose.

She pressed her fingertips to her mouth until she could speak. "I wish I'd been able to back off," she whispered, "handle my own fear better. I can't undo it. But he didn't leave to escape me, Molly. He left to escape himself."

"I would have reminded him about his life jacket—" My throat felt raw and swollen. "You never loved him," I said.

She shook her head slowly. "Oh, Molly." Her eyes were filled with such sadness and loss, and such disappointment in me, that I ran to my cabin and slammed the door, trying to lock all the pain outside.

Later, Karl motored up in the dinghy with Elizabeth and Jason to pick me up. My mother tapped on my door, but I wiggled out of my hatch. She joined me on deck, but I avoided her eyes.

"I'll drop the kids off" Karl said, "and come back to give you a hand with the outboard. Risa is sending a launch for the rest of us in a little while."

I scanned the anchorage once before climbing into the dinghy, but still no Christopher. *He has to come*, I thought.

Jason said, "We have our own room, Molly. Risa said we could share one."

"Hello. Earth to brother," Elizabeth said. "Molly and *I* are staying in the room. Brothers always stay in the yard during hurricanes. It's a rule."

He grinned at me and flipped his shark, but I had no patience for his silliness.

My mother handed down the overnight bag I'd forgotten. She started to speak, then stiffened in anger. I followed her eyes toward the harbor entrance.

Christopher had finally arrived.

"What is wrong with him," my mother said, "getting here so late? He'll end up putting other boats in jeopardy. I hope he has brains enough to get off that boat at least."

Before he even anchored, he scanned the shoreline, then *Emerald Eyes*, with binoculars. There was something different about his boat. I was trying to figure out what it was when he spotted me in the dinghy. He waved tentatively, never taking his eyes off me. He held his hands out in a questioning gesture. When my mother wasn't watching, I nodded. We would take care of each other, Christopher and I.

The only one who saw us was Elizabeth, and when she poked me with her elbow, I wouldn't meet her eyes.

My mother had made me think everyone would go ashore for the hurricane, and I was furious to see so many people remaining with their boats to keep them safe, people who weren't Nervous Nellies. How could this hurricane possibly be as bad as she feared? All the way to shore I stared at *Emerald Eyes*, tried to memorize everything about her. The shiny white hull and green trim, the sweetness of her lines, and my father at the helm, smiling, full of life. Tied into the mangroves with so many lines, she looked like a beautiful dragonfly, bending the water, about to fly away.

The streets were busy with shopkeepers boarding up their storefronts, when we stopped for last-minute food and supplies. Goats wandered through the square, and children tried to herd them back to their pens. Cars and pickups were laden with belongings as people moved from their low-lying homes to stay with friends and relatives in the hills or at the schools that would be used as shelters.

Several West Indian families, employees and Risa's friends, were already at the hotel when we arrived. They were tossing lawn furniture into the pool so it wouldn't blow away. Jason ran up to one of the Great Danes, and it took a wet swipe at his face with its long tongue. Honey Man crept on his belly toward some wild game he imagined in the tall grass that bordered the property.

The weather was perfect. The sun shone brightly through a fluffy spattering of clouds, and a gentle breeze blew blossoms along the ground. It seemed impossible that a hurricane was roaring toward us.

We left everyone at the hotel and ran to Risa's house, the dogs cantering at our heels, to help drag redwood furniture inside. There were cottages on the property, but no one was staying in them because of their flimsy sheet-metal roofs. The hotel and Risa's house were supposed to be safer because of the hurricane shutters on the windows and the heavily constructed roofs. My stomach was twisted with anxiety, and I pressed my hands against it. Would I find a chance to get away? Did I really want to? Waiting for a chance to talk to me, Elizabeth never left my side.

When the palm fronds began to rattle, when the wind began to stir like a jungle cat shaking itself awake, I knew I didn't want to go.

Risa ran out of the house yelling, "Honey Man!" She had just done a cat count and discovered he was missing.

"I'll look for him!" I yelled.

Elizabeth took off after me.

The wind shook the trees, and brilliant red flowers blew across the lawn like a brush fire. I was halfway down the hill before Elizabeth caught up with me.

"Where are you going?" she said breathlessly.

I stared at her but couldn't speak.

She grabbed my arms. "What are you doing?"

"I have to protect *Emerald Eyes*."

"No, Molly. You can't do that. You have to stay here."

I kept backing up, and she kept following me. Her eyes were shiny and frightened. "Why are you doing this?" she asked. And the truth is, I didn't know why. It was as if a storm was raging inside of me, a storm as dangerous as the one approaching. The wind snapped my beaded braid across my face. "Don't tell on me."

"Don't ask me that, Molly, please."

"I'll just check on the boat, okay. I'll come back in a little while, I promise." I turned and raced down the hill.

Once I looked back, but Elizabeth was already gone.

Fourteen

CHRISTOPHER WASN'T WAITING ON SHORE when I got there, but when he spotted me, he jumped right into his dinghy. "I almost gave up on you," he said. The relief in his eyes was so great that I thought I'd made the right decision.

A gust of wind blew under the bow of the light inflatable and almost flipped us over. Christopher threw himself on the bow, and I took the tiller and steered toward *Sinbad*. Approaching the boat, I suddenly knew what had troubled me since finding Christopher in the cove: He said he was getting the boat ready in case they went to sea. But why was he bothering to *paint* it to face a hurricane? I'd assumed he was painting the scrape on the hull, but as we neared, I saw it hadn't been touched. Yet something about the boat was different.

"I have to set more anchors," he cried over the wind. I scrambled aboard and ran to release the starboard anchor while Christopher stood in the dinghy under the bow. His was the only boat in the harbor with only one anchor set, and the memory of my mother's anger chafed at my mind. The boat was pitching, and the anchor jammed. "Hurry up!" he yelled. Finally it lowered into the dinghy. He tried to motor out with it while I fed him line, but the wind was increasing rapidly. When he finally dropped it over, I knew it wasn't out nearly as far as it should be.

We tried the same drill with another anchor. I was unfamiliar with the boat, and the line snagged on a cleat. The boat heeled, knocking me off balance. Angrily Christopher yelled, "Will you hurry it up? I'll never get anchored at this rate."

"It's not my fault you got here at the last minute!"

The wind was blowing so hard, he couldn't make any headway in the dinghy. I had to raise the anchor back onto the deck. I lost my footing when the boat lurched, smashing my toe. Tears of pain filled my eyes.

Boat rigging whistled throughout the anchorage. I'd been in one hurricane on Long Island when I was little, and already I knew Hurricane Hank was different. It was still miles and miles away, yet we couldn't stand on deck without having to bend into the wind. A tree branch blew through the air and slammed onto a nearby boat. The people aboard rushed below. I watched Christopher's face as he tried to clear the deck of equipment. The wind pulled his lips over his teeth in an eerie grin. His eyes were wild. I looked back up the hill and saw heavy branches blowing around like giant tumbleweed. I wondered if my mother was searching for me. I closed my eyes against the image and the biting wind.

Christopher rushed up to me with two pieces of hose. "Get these on the anchor lines for me while I tie the mainsail on the boom." I ran to the bow and bent the heavy rubber around the lines so they wouldn't wear through. I almost lost a finger when a blast of wind increased tension on the line. My fear was building with the storm.

The wind was so intense I had to clutch the lifelines as I walked back to keep from blowing overboard. "Why did you wait so long to get here?" I didn't care that I sounded like my mother. His carelessness had put us both in danger.

"I had to wait for the Coast Guard to leave!" Christopher stopped moving—as if he realized he'd made a serious mistake.

"Why did you have to wait for them to leave?" A warning clanged in my mind. Instantly I knew why the boat looked different: The waterline stripe was a different color! I remembered my father telling me that smugglers raised the stripe when extra weight was on board. Otherwise the boat would look suspiciously low in the water. Was the waterline stripe only a different color? Or was it higher than before?

"Why are you afraid of the Coast Guard, Christopher?"

"Help me tie this sail onto the boom!" He avoided my eyes.

I grabbed his arm. "Answer me." He shrugged it away.

"Are you going to help me or give me a hard time?" He didn't look young and vulnerable anymore. He looked like an angry stranger.

"What about *Emerald Eyes*?" I cried. He ignored me and kept lashing the sail.

"Christopher? Aren't you going to help me with *Emerald Eyes*?"

"Your boat's fine," he said, not looking at me. "I'm the one who needs help, not you! Finish securing this sail while I tie off the halyards."

White water blew across the harbor like snow in a raging blizzard. I stared at *Emerald Eyes* in amazement. It was as if the howling wind had blown away the fog of grief, allowing me to see clearly for the first time. The boat was secure in a narrow mangrove channel, as far away from other boats as my mother could put it. She had done everything possible to protect the boat. To protect her family. A gust of wind almost knocked me over, and I realized my mother was right: The hurricane hadn't even hit yet and I could hardly stand on deck. There was nothing I could do to save *Emerald Eyes*. And now I wasn't sure I could save myself.

"Don't just stand there!" Christopher yelled.

I heard an urgent voice in my mind, in my heart: *Get away, McGoo. Now! Go back to your mother.* So much became clear to me. There was no hidden meaning behind my father's last gift. He gave me the book only because he knew I'd enjoy it. Daddy would *never* want me to sail away alone, to sail away from my mother.

I shouted at Christopher, "Take me back to shore! You never intended to come over to my boat with me, did you? You just needed me to help you." He kept working without answering.

The wind began to scream. A violent gust lifted me off my feet, and I slid along the deck.

"Take me back to my mother!"

Tied to the stern, the dinghy flipped upside down and back again. The outboard hung by one bolt, and when the dinghy flipped again, the motor fell off and sunk. The lightened inflatable began spinning from the stern like a pinwheel. The line snapped and the dinghy flew away.

There was no way to get off the boat.

In horror, I watched a wooden fishing boat drag across

the harbor and slam into a catamaran. Another sailboat floated into the shallows and flopped on its side.

"Why did you wait until the Coast Guard left?" I punched his arm over and over. He kept working, refusing to look at me, his eyes filled with panic.

A cushion sailed through the air and smacked me in the ear. I almost fell overboard. Christopher grabbed me and helped me below. The cabin was cavernous and empty. No pictures hanging up. No books lining the shelves. There was nothing personal in the whole cabin. It wasn't a home. What was it? I pulled away from him.

"Where is Turner? Tell me the truth."

"What do you mean? I told you—"

"Stop lying!"

He held the top of his head with both hands. "Turner went to another island about something . . . where he owns a house . . . and he got arrested. I was stuck and needed help."

I glared at him. "Why did you have to wait for the Coast Guard to go?"

He hesitated. "I swear, Molly, I was going over to your boat to help you." Looking into his eyes, I remembered the first time I'd ever met him. He was a good liar then. And he was a good liar still.

"Why did you paint the waterline stripe?" Even as I asked, I knew he'd painted a higher stripe so the Coast Guard wouldn't notice that the boat was weighted down by heavy cargo. I started yanking lockers open. How long had I known? Since I'd seen the drug boat speeding to Aves Island? Since I'd heard the plane flying low without lights? Or had I known something was wrong from the first time I saw him?

Christopher grabbed my wrist to stop me.

Sinbad was lunging, straining to get free. Suddenly, there was no resistance. The boat felt like it was racing through the water. Our anchors had torn loose. Were we blowing out to sea or toward shore? The wind was screeching in the rigging. A boat hit us and I was thrown to the floor. It came from above like a rogue whale. The deck above my head cracked open.

A second boat slammed into us moments later. It chewed at the bow, and water gushed in through a ragged hole. We hit bottom. *Sinbad* rolled over on her side like a wounded whale. The other boats tore into her and ripped great chunks away from her body. I fell on my back against a bulkhead as floorboards broke loose and barely missed my head. Heavy bales wrapped in black plastic spilled from the bilges and forward cabin and pinned me at the waist. I remembered the bale of marijuana found floating at Aves Island. I screamed for my mother, but couldn't hear my voice above a raging gust of wind.

Christopher's face was white, terror in his eyes. He tried to pull the bales of marijuana from my body. "Oh, God, I'm sorry," he said. I was sobbing, furious at him and at myself. He never intended to help me protect *Emerald Eyes*. He just needed someone to help him keep his drugs safe.

"Molly, I'm sorry." He tore at the bales, trying to get them off me. "I didn't expect the hurricane. The stuff should have been sold already, but the Coast Guard—" The boat shuddered, and a bale hit my leg, twisting my knee. "I'll get you free, don't worry—" He started rambling like he needed to convince himself that he'd done the right thing. "Don't you see? With Turner busted, I could make some real money instead of the lousy cut he was giving me to help him. I just wanted a good boat, pick up the kids, sail them around the world—"

"Get these things off me! I want my mother," I cried.

"It was my one big chance! I canceled Turner's deal and made a better one. I'm a dead man if I lose the dope. I needed help, Molly. I'm sorry." Christopher strained at the bales, but something had me pinned and he couldn't budge it. Water was sloshing around me, the wind steadily increasing.

The boat was on its side, pounding the bottom. When it shuddered, my teeth rattled together. A mast from another boat pierced *Sinbad* like a spear, just missing my chest. Christopher pressed his mouth against my ear and shouted over the screaming wind, "I'll see if I can get help. I'm so sorry, Molly. I never thought it could be this bad." He turned back once, and his eyes were wet with tears.

The bow of another boat ripped through our hull and shook violently like a shark with a piece of meat. Christopher crawled through a gaping wound in the hull. The wind slammed into his body and lifted him. Flapping in mid-air like a flag, he held on to a stanchion. One of his hands slipped free. Then the other. He turned his face to me as Hurricane Hank dragged his body away. Then the boat rolled and water rushed up to my neck.

I don't know when the wind died, leaving me trapped in an eerie silence. It seemed like I struggled forever, trying to hold my head above water as the boat settled lower and lower. I was afraid to move, afraid I'd cause the boat to roll over completely and bury me below the surface.

I'd prayed so hard for my mother I thought I was dreaming when I heard her shout my name.

I tipped my head back as far as it would go, blowing water away from my mouth. Again and again, I heard my mother call my name. I drew on the last of my strength and cried out, but my voice was barely a whisper. Bits of wreckage fell into the boat as someone crawled above me. Then I saw my mother's face, saw the fierceness of her love.

"Mommy," I said in a small voice.

"Molly," she whispered, muddy tears streaking her face. "Molly, oh my God. Oh, sweetheart. It's okay now, honey. I'm here. I'll get you out."

She jumped into the water through the broken hull and dived under, tearing at the bales and wreckage that had me trapped. She broke the surface over and over for air, but kept diving, kept ripping at the terrible weight holding me down. And I knew as I watched her, knew in the deepest part of my heart, that my mother would protect me like she always had. And even when the boat began to roll and my face slipped under water, even then, when the last bit of air had left my lungs, I knew my mother would set me free.

The weight tumbled from my body. We broke through the surface together, and I threw my arms around her neck. We held onto each other, gasping, sobbing.

Roger appeared above us. His eyes widened when he saw the bales.

They pulled me through the hull and helped me to my feet, my legs cramped, my knee aching.

"We have to hurry, Molly," Roger said. "We're in the eye of the storm."

We climbed over mounds of debris to get to shore. I felt

confused and wondered where I was. I didn't see *Emerald Eyes*. I thought I saw a horse lying on its side, a white star on its forehead. There were no boats left in the middle of the lagoon. Roger tried to pull me up the hill, but I wouldn't let go of my mother. She guided me, her arm tightly around my shoulder.

A gentle breeze blew. The sun drifted through clouds. I was tired and I stumbled in pain. Roger kept looking over his shoulder like we were being followed. He ran ahead and pulled on the front door of one of the cottages. It flew open. He hurried Mom and me inside and pushed us into the bathroom. He stuffed blankets and pillows into the tub with us. Then he sat on the floor and rested his head on his knees while we waited for the eye to pass.

Hank roared to life with a vengeance.

I held my hands against the pain in my ears. A violent whirlwind filled the room. Brown leaves exploded from nowhere and stuck to the walls like dead moths. The house shook. The door jamb splintered as the living room sofa tore into the bathroom like an animal trying to devour us. Mom screamed, and the deafening howl of the storm roared from her mouth. I closed my eyes and slipped into darkness.

Fifteen

THE ISLAND WAS A DRY, BROWN HUSK.

We stood in the rubble, Roger, Mom, and me, looking out at a wasteland. No flowers, a few dead leaves hanging from broken branches on the burnt lawn. Furniture from three of Risa's cottages lay tangled in mahogany and gumbo-limbo trees that were cracked and partially uprooted. Some trees stood like bare poles, every branch torn away. A mattress hung over the side of the swimming pool, now filled with dark, muddy water. Honey Man sat on a television in the middle of the lawn, licking one of his paws.

When the wall of the storm hit, after the eye passed over, the cottage we were in lost its roof suddenly, and furniture was sucked up and blown through the house. The storm raged for five more hours. No one at Risa's house or the hotel had been injured. Most of the homes on the island were seriously damaged. It was a miracle that none of the islanders were killed.

We went out to the boats together late in the afternoon. *Magic* was still seaworthy, but her starboard rail was slightly damaged, a stanchion torn lose. Another boat had dragged on top of *Dreamer* and put a big hole in her middle. Peter and Theresa wouldn't have to sell her after all—she was a total loss. *Golden Slippers* was injured, too. Both of her masts dangled in half like fractured bones.

I stared at *Emerald Eyes*. Covered with dead leaves, her white cabin was stained pink, as though the tree roots had bled. She was tied securely into the mangroves, safe and undamaged, bobbing peacefully where my mother had anchored her.

Most of the people who stayed on their boats survived, a few did not. One man who tried to get off his boat had been killed on land by flying debris when the eye passed over. Someone else had died of a heart attack. The catamaran was floating upside down, its mast stuck in the mud below. Its young captain had managed to stay alive in an air pocket when the boat flipped. He had seen his wife washed away.

And Christopher. His body was found tangled in the mangrove roots near shore. He is now buried in a small cemetery on the island, near a flamboyant tree that will bloom again and spill red blossoms on his grave. His mother came alone to the funeral. One thing Christopher hadn't lied about was having a little brother and sisters. I will always believe he wanted to buy a boat—to sail them around the world.

I thought I might get arrested for being on a boat with drugs, but the Coast Guard knew I wasn't involved. Elizabeth had looked scared and guilty when I first saw her. "Molly, I told your mother where you were," she said. "You should have seen her. I had to tell her. But they couldn't look for you until the eye came over." When I told her everything, about Christopher and my father, we hugged each other so hard, I thought we'd never let go.

Roger arranged to have *Golden Slippers* shipped back to Maryland on a freighter two weeks later, so he could repair it properly at his father's boat yard. We remained at Manchioneel until he left, helping Risa and other islanders. The crane lifted his sailboat, like a wounded patient, and lowered her gently onto a ship.

We went to the airport with him. Several broken planes were still swept together near the edge of a torn chain-link fence. The hot air shimmered above the runway.

"Well," he said. "I guess I won't see you for a while." He pulled something from his canvas bag. "This is for you, Molly."

Shyly, he shook my mother's hand. "I'll write. Maybe I'll sail back to the Caribbean when *Golden Slippers* is repaired." My mother smiled and hugged him. And so did I.

Roger had offered to sail with us to Florida, but Mom and I weren't ready to sell the boat. And we weren't ready to bring anyone into our lives. Not even someone as special as Roger. For now, we would sail *Emerald Eyes* together—just the two of us—one day at a time.

I opened his gift. All the time I had been frightened and hurt, watching him stare over at us, he'd been drawing a sailboat with a girl and a woman at the helm, my mother and me. *Emerald Eyes* was following the silver wake of dolphins. In the sky, he'd painted stars that shone like diamond chips. But near the Big Dipper, the North Star was a sparkle of green, my father watching from heaven.

Mom and I stood on the hot tarmac, her arm around

my shoulder, until Roger's plane became a tiny speck in the sky and disappeared.

Elizabeth and Jason wave their wands on *Magic*, as we sail down-island for the rest of hurricane season. Their bubbles dance around my mother's head like a halo while she reads her daily meditation out loud. She says it will help me understand that it wasn't her fault my father went away. And it wasn't my fault he died. My mind already knows this is true. And Mom says in time my feelings will catch up. We don't blame Daddy for anything either. His alcoholism was like a lion, sleeping in the midst of our lives. When Uncle Frank died, it stirred and padded silently toward my father, and Daddy forgot that he needed help to stay alive.

I close my eyes and feel the wind on my face, feel my father's lips brush my forehead. I should have known before my mother told me: Daddy didn't want to take me with him on the sailing trip. Sober, he wouldn't even consider it. Their raised voices had been my mother pleading with him not to leave us. But Mom couldn't hold off my father's disease, any more than I could hold back the storm that claimed Christopher.

Often I think about Christopher. How different his life might have been if he'd had parents like mine to love him. Sometimes I picture him happy and whole, like that first time I saw him. Windsurfing, leaning away from the sail to pick up speed. But always when I think of him, he heads for the reef, skims over the top safely, and races by me. And always, I whisper, "*Yeah.*"

Dolphins leap and streak across our bow, leaving a

wake of pure silver. The warm trade wind lifts my mother's soft brown hair, sweeping it around her face, her amber eyes gentle with love for me and Daddy. *Emerald Eyes* leans into the wind as the crimson sun sinks slowly in the west. *She's getting close, McGoo.* Then the earth tips and a green flash bursts on the very edge of the sea. My father's Irish laughter is the wind.